Flippin' Fairies

A Flippin' Anthology Volume 1

Edited by Rob Goodale

Chaos and Ink Books, LLC

Flippin' Fairies: A Flippin' Anthology Volume 1

Book Cover and Interior Illustrations Designed by S. L. Black

Frolickin' Fairies Art by Katie Shaw

Contents

Frolickin' Fairies by Katie Shaw

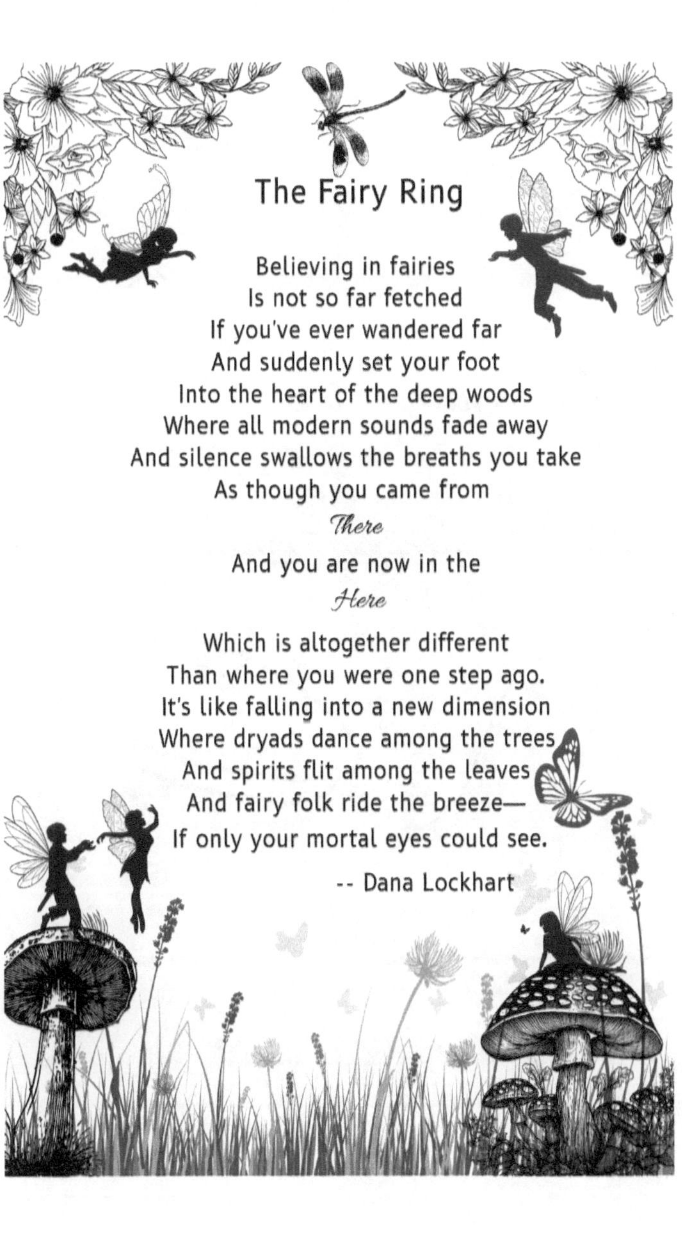

The Fairy Ring

Believing in fairies
Is not so far fetched
If you've ever wandered far
And suddenly set your foot
Into the heart of the deep woods
Where all modern sounds fade away
And silence swallows the breaths you take
As though you came from
There

And you are now in the
Here

Which is altogether different
Than where you were one step ago.
It's like falling into a new dimension
Where dryads dance among the trees
And spirits flit among the leaves
And fairy folk ride the breeze—
If only your mortal eyes could see.

-- Dana Lockhart

Missing Pieces

by
Ashley Wong

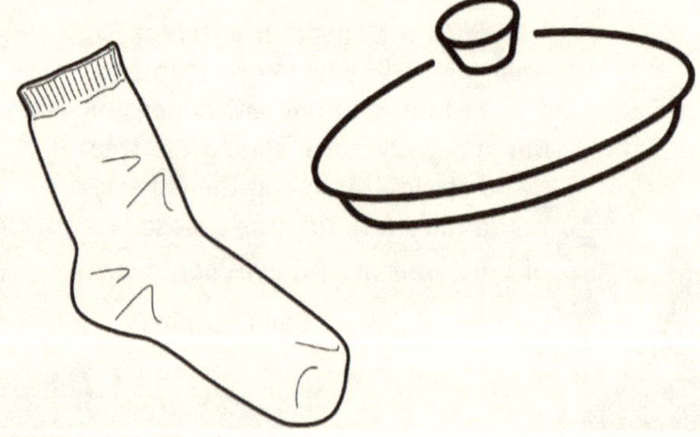

I stared at the sock sticking to the bottom of the washer and sighed. Looks like I'm going in after it. Being only 5'2" meant I had to hoist myself into the washer headfirst, pelvic bone digging into the edge of the machine and feet dangling inches above the floor. I stretched my arm, reaching for the sock. At the exact moment my hand grasped the damp cotton, I felt a tug and I was falling.

I braced myself to hit the hard metal, thinking I had just become unbalanced, but I went right through the bottom of the washer. My hand gripped the sock for dear life as it tugged me along through cold, dark air.

I heard a gasp as I came to a surprisingly soft landing.

"Oh no, oh no. You're not supposed to be here. What have I done? What do I do?" a voice muttered.

A girl, who was smaller than me by half, paced in front of me. I thought it was the dim lighting, but her skin looked tinged with blue.

"Where am I?" I asked the girl.

"Shhhh...if they hear you, they will want to keep you. Quickly, follow me. And do try to stay quiet," the girl said.

Now that I looked closer, she wasn't exactly a girl. I followed her, anyway. What choice did I have?

The ground was soft, like walking on a floor of pillows. It looked like thick grass, or maybe moss. Our steps didn't make a sound. But I did hear something, a quiet fluttering. It was then that I noticed them.

Scattered throughout the woods around us were what looked, at first glance, like fireflies. They didn't come close, but I could see their tiny bodies outlined by the glow of their wings. They looked like miniature pastel Barbie dolls dressed in delicate flower petals.

"Fairies," I whispered.

At once, they scattered, as if blown back by a gust of wind.

"Pixies, actually. I'm a fairy," the girl replied.

I turned my attention back to her and took in the details of her appearance. She had wings also, but they were translucent and didn't flutter while she walked, making them hard to see. Her ears were pointed, and I was pretty sure now that her skin was a pale blue. Her clothes were vines and large leaves.

"There we are. Hurry along," the *fairy* said as she opened a door set into a large tree and stepped inside.

I had to crouch to fit through the door. Once inside, I was able to stand, barely. My head was inches from the ceiling. I chuckled; I finally knew what it felt like to be tall.

The room was lit by glowing orbs that were set into stems dangling from the ceiling. The furniture looked carved from the tree itself, everything seamlessly connecting to the floors and walls. Chairs and a table grew up from the floor, and cupboards and countertops sprouted from the walls.

"Where am I?" I asked the fairy.

"I thought that would be obvious. You're in Elfhame, the land of fairies."

"The land of fairies is in my laundry room?"

"No, silly," the fairy said with a laugh like a wind chime. "Elfhame is just another location in your world, but it's disguised to humans. The land of fairies exists all around you, but humans cannot enter unless a fairy brings them here." A frown scrunched up her pretty face. "I didn't mean to bring you here."

I opened my mouth to ask why she didn't send me back, but I hesitated. If I brought it up, she might send me back now. This is the fairy world! I wanted a chance to explore it before I had to go home. I only got a glimpse of this land on the way here. Which reminded me...

"Who are we hiding from? You said they would want to '*keep me*'."

"The Fae," she whispers with a shiver. "They are the only ones that like to take humans. We fairies frown on that. We tend to stick to items." She holds up my soggy sock as proof. "I promise I didn't mean to take you. You just had a hold on the sock when I pulled it through." She pouts and shifts her feet.

"Ummm...it's ok," I tell her, trying to smile reassuringly.

"You're not mad?" she asks.

"No, I'm not mad." Mad is one of the few emotions I don't feel right now.

The little fairy beams up at me and her wings flutter.

"Wait, why did you take my sock, anyway?" I ask.

"It was left in the bottom of the wash. I didn't think it would be an inconvenience."

"I mean, what would you want with my sock?"

"Oh, it's to power our magic."

"You power your magic with socks?" I scoff.

"We use lots of things: Tupperware lids, puzzle pieces, gloves," she pauses. "And some use humans. Anything that's a part of a pair or a piece of something will do."

"But why would Fae use humans when a sock will do?"

"Oh, using humans is much more powerful. They are missed far more than a sock. Eventually, you throw out the other sock. But humans never forget their loved ones."

I let the truth of those words sink in. A second later, something clicked.

"You're saying there are people trapped here, and their loved ones don't know where they are?"

"Well... yes," she says, as she looks away.

"We've got to help them."

"What? We can't. It's simply not possible to help them." The fairy's cheeks flush. "I'm sorry," she adds. "I like humans, I do. I'd never take one myself, but the Fae are strong, and they do what they like."

"There's got to be a way. Will you please tell me how?" I ask.

At that moment, a glowing pixie floated in through an open window carved into the tree. Her skin is lavender, and her hair is like pink cotton candy.

"I wasn't eavesdropping, I promise. I just happened to be flying by, and this human voice caught my attention," the pixie says. "But we've got to help her, Erissa. The wee folk always help humans in need. That's what sets us apart from the cruel Fae."

The fairy, Erissa, begins shaking. "Oh, Belle, I know you're right, but what chance do we have against them?"

"We've got to stand up to them at some point. Maybe this human was meant to find us. Be brave, Erissa," Belle said.

The fairy looked between me and the pixie, and then she straightened. "We're going to need a lot more socks."

It didn't take much to disguise me as a Fae. Erissa used some magic to make my ears pointy and give my skin a pale shimmer. For her part, Belle stole some elegant Fae garments. Apparently, pixies were known to be mischievous, and the Fae wouldn't find it suspicious for clothing to vanish.

The dress I wore was a thin, airy fabric the color of a plum, with a golden belt cinching it to my waist. Belle wove golden leaves through my auburn hair, and the effect was striking. I suspected Erissa's magic had also given me this otherworldly beauty as I gazed in a mirror.

"You're ready," said Erissa. "I'll lead the way."

We stepped out of the tree house and into the dim morning light. I took in my surroundings as we walked. Throughout the forest, many trees had doors set into them, indicating a home. Glowing orbs, like the ones hanging from Erissa's ceiling, sparked to life as we walked. Bursts of colorful flowers sprouted up as we walked by, and the blooms closed once we moved past.

I looked down at Erissa. "Why is it that everything seems to come alive as we reach it?" I asked.

"Magic powers everything in our world. It's similar to electricity in your world. That's why we need to keep taking items from humans to replenish our supply. I only take what I need for my little home, but the Fae like extravagance. You'll see," Erissa said.

"Also, you might not want to speak once we get there," Belle said. "Your voice is rough and will certainly stand out."

I gaped at her. But my voice did sound rough compared to their sing-song voices.

It wasn't long before I saw what I could only assume was the territory of the Fae. The fairies made their homes inside the trees, but the Fae sat atop them like open-air palaces. Large branches created archways and bridges, linking close-knit trees that were larger than any I'd seen. The trunks were wide enough to serve as floors. Some rooms were closed off by partitions of vine and leaves. The furniture that I could see grew from the wood—similar to the fairy's—but these were polished and elaborate instead of simple carved pieces.

My awe turned to disgust when I remembered that this was all fueled by captive people. My anger made me unafraid as I followed Erissa and Belle into the Unseelie Court.

I kept my head held high as we wove through the massive treetop palace, passing Fae and fairies alike. Erissa stopped at the top of a staircase that led down into the base of a massive tree trunk. As we stepped down the staircase, I braced myself for the sight of imprisoned people in a miserable dungeon. But I wasn't prepared for what I saw.

The so-called dungeon was like the most lavish hotel in a magical land. People lounged on soft beds piled with pillows, leafy canopies affording them privacy when they slept. Mismatched pieces of fancy furniture were set around the open space to create living spaces. They looked stolen from mansions throughout the ages, each piece from a different time period with a mind to bring a familiar comfort to the humans. Vegetables, nuts, and berries piled high on tables. Pitchers of juices and wine sat next to wooden goblets. My jaw dropped as I took it all in.

Gradually, people began to notice us and stopped what they were doing to stand and face us. They looked like they were waiting for instructions. It was then I remembered that I looked like a Fae.

"Oh, umm, I'm not actually a Fae. I'm a human, and I'm here to rescue you," I said.

The people looked between each other, some wary and others curious. I scanned their faces, my gaze falling on a girl who looked at me with a glimmer of hope.

"I can take you home to your families," I said, looking at the girl.

She gulped. "How?"

"I can create a portal to send you home. I have magic, like the Fae. We just have to get you out of the palace first," Erissa spoke up.

"Do you expect a group of humans to just walk out of here? And how do we know this isn't a trick? She doesn't look human," a man said.

"I can show you. I just need a volunteer," Erissa replied.

"I'll do it." The hopeful girl stepped forward.

Erissa created the same pointy-eared, shimmery look that she did for me. A murmur of excitement spread through the room and others stepped forward. Soon, it looked like we were all ready to make our escape. But I noticed a teenage boy sitting alone at the back of the room.

"Are you ready to get transformed?" I asked him. "I think you're the last one."

"I don't want to," he said.

"It doesn't hurt. I promise," I replied.

"No," he said with a frown, "I don't want to leave."

I stared at him for a moment. "Why wouldn't you want to go home? Your parents must really miss you," I tried.

"This place is better than my home." He crossed his arms and looked away. "My parents...well, they don't miss me."

I didn't know this boy's parents or what his life was like at home, so I didn't try to convince him that his home was better. I thought quickly. I couldn't leave this boy here to miss his only chance to come back to the human world, at least not without being certain.

"I'm sure there is someone that you would like to see again," I said.

I scanned his face, and I saw it light up for a brief moment. But he shook his head.

"I mean, there is a girl, but I don't think she misses me. We've never even hung out outside of work."

"I know she misses you," I told him.

He glanced at me skeptically.

"I know," I continue, "because you're still here. The Fae wouldn't have any need for you unless someone in the human world missed you."

The boy looked at me longer this time and something in my gaze must have convinced him. He stood up and walked over to Erissa.

"I'm ready."

I sauntered up the stairway, casually looking around to make sure the way was clear. I turned and nodded to Erissa before continuing on. Belle flew beside me, showing me the way out. Erissa sent a handful of people to follow a few steps behind. She made sure everyone spread out so that it didn't appear suspicious. Afterwards, she would bring up the rear and make sure no one got lost.

I walked down the hall at an agonizingly slow pace. I wanted to run out of this palace, but I knew I had to set an example. Whenever I passed a real Fae, my heart skipped a beat. Still, I nodded my head and touched two fingers to my forehead in the greeting that Belle had taught me. So far, everyone had returned the gesture and no one seemed to notice anything amiss.

Erissa had explained that the Fae shouldn't be able to detect the humans' absence until we crossed over the border of the Unseelie Court. At that point, they would be alerted by the significant loss of magic, like how we only notice a power outage because things turn off. When that happened, we needed to run. I only hoped they didn't figure out right away which way we had gone.

Belle stopped and held out a hand to signal for me to stop. We had reached the border, but we couldn't cross until the others caught up. I had to ensure we all had enough time to make it out.

I leaned casually against a tree branch banister and started chatting with the group that came up behind me. They played along, making sure not to step onto the staircase leading down from the trees. From the looks of it, Belle had taken us to an entrance that wasn't frequently used. Pretty soon, we had a large group gathered and I knew we would stand out if anyone came by. I silently urged the others along, trying not to look antsy. I sighed when I saw Erissa trailing behind the last cluster of people.

Then, I saw a Fae approaching us from another direction. I glanced back to Erissa. I didn't know what to do. If we took off running when the rest of the group arrived, this Fae could give chase or alert the other Fae to our location. We needed to convince her that nothing was unusual.

The Fae woman's eyes roamed the group as she walked closer and her brows scrunched together. I tried to think of a reason for such a large gathering near an exit. Erissa and the rest of the group were nearing and I hoped no one would panic. And then, I thought of our excuse.

I turned to the approaching group and yelled, "Happy Birthday!"

I only hoped the Fae celebrated birthdays like humans did. The others caught on and a chorus of enthusiastic "Happy Birthdays" rang out. When the Fae walked past, I smiled in that apologetic way you do when your friends are causing a ruckus and touched my fingers to my forehead. The Fae smiled back and returned the greeting.

We all kept up the hugs and chatter until the Fae woman was out of sight. We gave her a few minutes to make sure she was far enough away before we crossed the border. Belle told the group to follow her glowing wings as fast as they could and flew off.

We raced down the stairs after her and Erissa, who tried to fly at a pace we could keep up with. It was obvious the

Fae would catch us, if they knew where to look. It was important that we make it into the forest quickly.

For a few tense moments, it was only pounding feet and the sharp intake of breath. At last, we were out of the clearing and under the shade of dense vegetation. But we couldn't stop yet.

Erissa had picked out a spot that would be far enough into the woods to hide what she would have to do. We continued running after her until she stopped ahead and began tracing markings along the ground. The last of the group caught up to us right as she seemed to finish and turned to look around. That's when her eyes went wide.

I looked behind us to see a group of Fae sprinting toward us. They were unearthly fast. Erissa flew into the air and began muttering rapidly above the markings. Then she opened her eyes.

"Go," she yelled as a portal swirled to life behind her.

I didn't even pause to say goodbye. I leapt through the portal, hoping the others would make it.

"Ugh, I still can't find the match to this sock," my sister cries out. "I'm just going to throw it out."

"Don't do that," I say with a fond smile, thinking of my friend Erissa. "Just hold on to it. You never know when that sock might turn up."

My sister sighs and stuffs the sock back into her drawer. I consider that deed a small measure of repayment for all the lives saved by a scared little fairy.

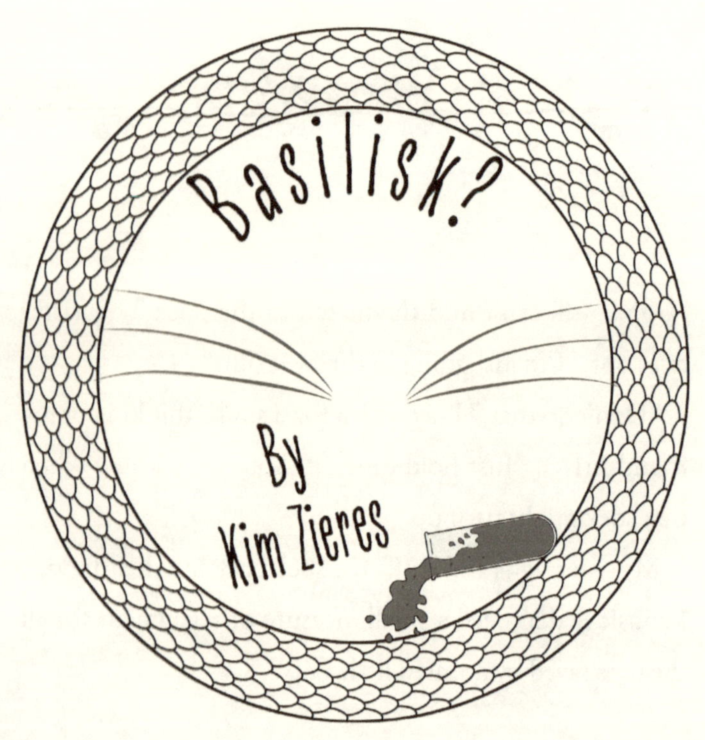

Basilisk?
By
Kim Zieres

"Grandma, Grandma!!!! Did you hear!? Daddy said there's a bad Grym on the loose out at the state park!"

Kornelia smiled fondly as her 5-year-old great-granddaughter practically tumbled through the door of her kitchen. Elora's presence meant Kornelia had missed the sound of the school bell ringing down the street. At nearly 78 years of age, maybe it was time to get her hearing checked.

"Why, hello to you, too, Elora," Kornelia greeted her. "There are peanut butter cookies in the cookie jar. Grab us each 2 and we'll discuss your news over a cold glass of milk. How many cookies do you need if we each get 2?"

Elora climbed onto her customary stool and started pulling the cookies from the jar shaped like a faerie dragon sleeping on a hoard of cookies that sat on the counter. She stopped for a moment to count on her fingers before responding.

"Four!"

"Good job, dear."

They settled onto their stools and for a moment, the only sounds were those of enjoyment as they focused on their snack. When Elora broke the companionable silence, it was with one of her customary questions.

"Grandma, didn't you used to hunt bad Gryms?"

"That was a long time ago, dear," Kornelia replied. "I leave that to the professionals these days."

"Did you ever see a baskalesk?"

Kornelia hoped that Elora didn't hear the sudden catch in her voice. "As much as anyone can see a basilisk, dear. You can't look into their eyes."

"What do they look like?"

Kornelia thought back to that day. If Vera hadn't stepped in the way, Kornelia could have been the one lowered into the ground a few days later.

"They have a long body with scales like a snake, but the head and beak of a rooster. Do you remember what a rooster is?" Kornelia asked, shivering just a bit as she remembered the sound of an angrily clacking beak.

"A boy chicken," Elora cried.

"That's right." She continued, "They have wings like a chicken, but they can't fly. If you ever hear about a basilisk sighting, you stay far away, dear. Bad Gryms like that should be taken care of by professionals."

"Like my daddy!"

"Just like your daddy," Kornelia agreed. She purposefully left out just how dangerous a basilisk could be. No point in scaring her. From there, the conversation turned to the latest playground gossip and before either of them knew it, the kitchen door opened once again to admit

Elora's father, Hugo. He was wearing his work uniform, which could only mean one thing.

"Off to work, Hugo?" Kornelia asked as she handed him Elora's bookbag.

"Yeah, grandma. I've got to head to work as soon as I drop Elora at home," Hugo replied.

"Elora said there was a basilisk sighting. Don't forget to take weasel musk," she reminded him.

"I've got some in the emergency kit you gave me," he nodded. With that, he swept up Elora and the two of them headed back out the door.

The ringing of the phone woke her from her doze on the couch sometime later. She peered up at the clock and realized it was nearly 2 A.M.

"Stills residence. Can I help you?"

"Kornelia, it's Gus." He tried—and failed—to sound casual as he continued, "have you still got that old emergency kit you used to lug around"

"Yes, I have the kit; it never left my car. But, I'm old Gus, not stupid," she snapped. "You and I both know you'd never call this late if it weren't an emergency. Out with it!"

Gus sighed heavily. "Hugo and Arnie brought the basilisk in around midnight. It's down in the containment pens, but I think something is wrong. Arnie left after 20 minutes, but Hugo still hasn't come back. One of the containment alarms went off about 10 minutes ago."

"I'll be on the road in ten." Whatever reply Gus may have made was lost as she hung up the phone and rose to get her keys.

Kornelia gripped the steering wheel tightly as she navigated the windy country roads. She hated driving after dark these days, but she couldn't risk leaving Hugo in danger for however long it took the rescue team to arrive. She knew the route to the county's confinement facility well enough to let her mind wander. It had been more than 50 years since the last time she'd dealt with a basilisk. A minor tremble shook her hands as she remembered the aftermath. The tremble worsened as she pictured her cousin Vera's pale, lifeless form lying in that coffin. Tears tracked down her cheeks and she swiped at them before refocusing on the road. She could only hope the weasel musk in her emergency kit would subdue the thing until the federal containment team arrived.

The rest of the drive felt somehow the longest and shortest ten minutes she'd ever experienced. She pulled into the drive of the old repurposed warehouse and parked. The tremble in her hands was back as she pulled her emergency kit from the backseat and headed inside. Gus met her just past the reception desk.

"Kornelia," he began, reaching for the case in her hands. "I'll take the kit and handle it."

She quickly jerked the case out of his reach. "Besides Hugo and I, there isn't another handler for 200 miles that's trained to handle something as dangerous as this, Gus. I'll head down there myself, thank you."

"You can't be serious. I can't let you go in there," he exclaimed, moving into her path.

"Gus Whittle, you get out of my way this instant!" she replied.

"Hugo knows not to look at the thing. The feds will get here, and get him out soo- HEY!" he shouted the last in surprise as she used her cane to brush past him.

"The damn things are venomous, too, you idiot," she retorted. "You aren't trained for this."

She left him standing there in bewilderment as she hurried back to the area where Hugo should be. Her knees and hips ached as she navigated the steps to the sublevel. Finally, she caught sight of the glass enclosures, but an unexpected flash at ground level made her stop short. She stared numbly at the broken glass littering the floor for a moment, then snapped her eyes shut as she realized one of the enclosure walls must be broken. That explained the containment alarm Gus had mentioned.

It took her a moment of fumbling to find the right vial inside her bag. The braille on the label assured her of her success. She wondered again exactly what the weasel musk would do to the basilisk. They were incredibly rare, and she only knew of 3 other confirmed sightings in the last century.

A sudden, strange hissing noise sounded from behind her and she had to fight the urge to turn to meet it. She twisted open the vial in her hands instead. A nervous laugh tried to bubble its way up as she strained to hear the basilisk. *I'll call the doctor's office tomorrow and finally ask about hearing aids. As long as I haven't joined Vera by then.*

She kept the vial tightly clutched in one hand and reached for the wall she knew should be to her right. Once she found the wall, she put her back to it and slowly continued towards the enclosure door. The glass crunched underfoot, the pungent musk aroma assaulted her nostrils, and visions of Vera danced inside her eyelids. She forced herself onward. Hugo was her first grandchild. Nothing would stop her from finding him tonight.

Thankfully, it didn't take long. Her shuffling feet found him just inside the enclosure door. A frantic examination and a few desperate peeks through her slitted eyelids proved him alive but unconscious. She couldn't possibly lift him, and the nasty gash matting the hair on the back of his head meant he might not be awake for a while. Instead, she settled herself down next to him gingerly, her every joint protesting. At least his breathing was strong and steady.

Kornelia had just sat down when another sudden hiss startled her. She snapped her eyes open without thinking, but squeezed them shut again before catching more than a glimpse of scaly skin near the doorway. The acrid stench of the musk intensified as she splashed it in that direction. Claws scrabbling on the floor, the basilisk fled back down the hall.

The retreat surprised her a bit. Basilisks were normally very aggressive creatures, much more likely to spit their venom than run away. Maybe this one was sick? Gently moving her emergency bag from its position pillowed under Hugo's head, she sighed heavily before reaching inside.

The hand mirror was added to the kit years ago, but never believed she'd have to use it. She placed the mirror in her lap.

She moved to place the bag back underneath Hugo's head, and he moaned and began to thrash. Kornelia shook him, softly calling his name, but he didn't respond. Keeping her voice low, she began to sing a lullaby she'd sung to all of her children, grandchildren, and great-grandchildren. Her throaty, aged voice cracked at first, but gradually warmed to the melody. As it did so, Hugo's thrashing stilled, his breathing evened and his moans subsided.

A whisper of scales on cloth in the direction of Hugo's feet caught her attention. Her breath caught for a moment, and she was tempted to splash the remaining musk in that direction, but stopped when she realized how little was left in the vial. Only a direct hit had a chance to subdue the basilisk and for that, she would need to see it.

She lifted the hand mirror, angling it to catch a glimpse. At first, all she could see was a reflection of dirt-colored scales. Still singing softly so as not to startle the Grym, she tilted the mirror further.

Something seemed off about the way the stubby legs connected to the long, serpentine body. Off enough to make her delay using the musk for a second time. Her voice faltered, and she dropped the mirror as the creature suddenly crawled right up to her. She squeezed her eyes shut, but not before catching a glimpse of whiskers.

Warm, dry scales brushed against her hand, and a furry *something* pushed its way into her lap, knocking the vial from her hands. She froze in terror, sitting motionless as the weight settled in. Then a thought struck her.

Basilisks don't have fur.

Then a second thought. *Basilisks don't run away.*

Realization dawned on her with her third thought. *Basilisks don't have whiskers, either.*

Her trembling, seeking hands found warm furry ears near the top of what must be the head now in her lap. She knew she would find an identification tag in the left ear before her fingers touched it. With a deep, shaky breath, Kornelia opened her eyes.

When the rescue crew arrived several hours later, they were astonished to find Kornelia settled on the floor with the Grym's long snaky body loosely wrapped around her. It took a full 5 minutes of explaining before anyone from the team would even approach her. Even then, she had to give its furry feline face a good long stare before they would believe it wasn't a basilisk. She'd thought about giving it a kiss for good measure, but didn't think the team could stand the shock. The identification tag on its ear was the final piece to convince them. After the initial shock passed, Hugo seen by a medic, and the Grym safely stowed in a crate for transport, a woman with an air of authority approached Kornelia.

"You must be Mrs. Stills," the woman began. "I'm Veronica Marsh. I work for the Grym Deportation Facility. Mind filling me in on what's going on? That thing is obviously not a basilisk, so what is it?"

Veronica reached through the bars of the transport cage to give Mr. Whiskers a good scratch behind the ears. "I can see why there was confusion, though. On first glance, this cutie does look like the basilisk in the textbooks they make the handlers memorize these days."

"It's called a Tatzelwurm," Kornelia replied, "and we called him Mr. Whiskers." Veronica looked at her skeptically as she continued, "Tatzelwurms are even more rare than basilisks. This one is supposed to be living his best life in a preserve in the Swiss Alps. It's where I worked as a young woman. He was a tiny thing the last time I saw him. I used to sing him lullabies. He must have remembered them because they normally won't approach a human."

Veronica looked less skeptical and more puzzled as she asked her next question. "Any idea how it could have gotten all the way here to Idaho?"

Kornelia shook her head in dismay. "Not at all. But if the preserve isn't safe, what will you do with him now?"

"That depends on how dangerous he is, and if we can find a good handler for him. I doubt I have anyone well versed in creatures from that part of Europe." She grimaced. "Stupid budget cuts. If I can't find someone, I'll likely have to deport him back to the Grymveil."

"If you have someone who's willing, I'd be happy to train them," Kornelia volunteered. "I won't say he's not dangerous, because they can be if startled or cornered, but he was always sweet as pie as a baby once you earned his trust."

"I may take you up on that, Mrs. Stills. For now, why don't you get yourself to the medic and get warmed up? That ground had to be cold."

Kornelia nodded and walked over to join Hugo. After a quick exchange to ensure that Hugo would be fine, she decided it was time to finally head home.

The Wing Thief

by
Amber Leigh

There was a thief on the loose. They were large, wore attire that concealed themselves and would capture the delicate faeries and rip the wings off their bodies. Luckily for the faeries, their wings would grow back—more often than not. It was still quite bothersome, seeing as they couldn't fly for a few weeks, and even more bothersome that humans generally couldn't see faeries without some kind of magic. Wherever the thief left them, they were stuck until someone found them and alerted the others or they walked for hours back home.

The faeries had a system in place: they surrounded their land with magical runes that concealed them completely and some that would zap an intruder if they passed through their magic circles. If a faerie saw the thief or had their wings stolen, they would fire bright, colorful sparks into the sky to alert any other faeries nearby. Yet still, the thief would find a way and pluck their wings again and again. The faeries had had enough of this torture and decided it was time to fight back.

"Oh, what a beautiful pair!" the woman exclaimed as she moved the faerie wing earrings in the light. The sparkles were endless, as were the pastel colors—like a jewel in the morning sun.

"Yes, newly acquired." Said a raspy voice.

"Is it true these wings are imbued with magical properties?" The woman asked, blinking inquisitively at the seller.

"Indeed, they will bring you great luck, m'lady." The seller grinned with rotted teeth.

"I'll take them!" The woman excitedly handed the gruff man a handful of coins and skipped away happily.

By the end of the day, all the faerie wing jewelry had sold. The man was finishing closing the booth when the thief appeared, shrouded in dark cloth. The seller handed the thief a bulging sack of coins—their share of the sales. Acknowledging all the jewelry had sold, the thief promised to bring more soon. Faerie wing jewelry was extremely lucrative, indeed. With a wave of their hand, the thief disappeared into the night.

The faeries gathered in their largest hollowed-out tree stump for a meeting. Chatter filled the air as they found their places.

"The thief must be stopped!"

"How can the thief even find us?"

"It's time to fight back! Our numbers are far greater!"

"Settle down everyone, we shall discuss our next steps calmly and orderly!" Boomed the Head Faerie, silencing the chatter.

"We faeries are not perceivable by normal human eyes, which means no matter who the thief is, they are some sort of magic-wielding being."

"Yes! It must be an evil warlock!" A faerie chimed in.

"Perhaps…" Trailed the Head Faerie. "But there is another possibility."

The crowd hushed as the Head Faerie carried on.

"Long ago, there was a tale of a faerie who longed to be human. This faerie had fallen in love with a human, a human who could not see them." He paused for a few moments, his eyes revealing a deep and long-lingering sorrow.

"What happened to them?" Inquired a young faerie with bouncing red curls, not more than five years old.

The Head Faerie collected himself and continued, "The tale goes that the faerie flew to find a wizard who could transform them into a human. The wizard did just that, but what he did not tell the faerie was that they would live on far beyond the human, as the lifespan of a faerie is significantly longer. Though they did share a human's lifetime of love, their lover has long since died while the once-faerie lives on in a human world where all they know perishes."

"That's sad," said the little faerie matter-of-factly.

"Indeed, it is quite sad, little one," the Head Faerie responded with a pat on her head. "But, that once-faerie would know exactly where we dwell and would have all the means to be immune to our magical traps. Having lived an unnaturally long human life and watching all they love perish again and again may drive anyone mad."

"How do we stop them?" a lovely faerie with plush lips and flowing lavender hair asked.

"We must either fight to kill them, or find a wizard to change them back. If they are changed back, they will have nowhere to go, and we would need to welcome them with open arms back to our community." His stern gaze swept the curious crowd.

"What? After everything that thief has done to us? Not a chance!"

The gathered faeries began to rile with indecision.

With a motion of his hands, the Head Faerie calmed them once more.

"We must dig deep into our hearts and decide together. The choice is this: death or salvation."

After hours of heated debate, the faeries finally came to a decision of sorts. They would send out a group for reconnaissance to see if they could find a wizard willing to help them. They would travel to the nearest city of Alifen, which was full of magic-wielding beings and normal folk alike. Many lofty towers of marble and stone soared high into the sky. Magic flourished in this city.

The group of faeries was small and capable of flying to great heights. They weaved their way around the city, through numerous windows in various buildings and towers unnoticed, searching for the domain of a wizard. Finally, they reached a small room in one of the winding stone towers. Countless shelves of ingredients in glass bottles, wands, obsidian daggers, bundles of plants, and endless books and tomes radiating with magic energy filled the space.

"This has to be a wizard!" exclaimed a faerie with mint green flowing hair and copper eyes.

"Hello, friends," echoed a female voice.

The faeries startled, glancing around for the source of the voice. They heard a light chuckle as a woman with cascading dark hair came into view.

"I was just practicing an invisibility spell!" She chuckled again. "What are you guys doing in here?" she continued lightheartedly, as if faeries showing up unannounced was nothing new to her.

"We were searching for a wizard," the faerie with night-sky-colored hair responded, flicking his wings to stay just above the woman.

"Why do you need a wizard?" the woman asked as she turned to fiddle with her open book, most likely the one with the invisibility spell.

"Well…" The mint-haired faerie spoke up first after sharing a concerned glance. "It's a bit of a long story. We can just get out of your hair."

The faeries all turned to fly out of the window they came through.

"Wait! I'm a witch!" the woman said excitedly. "I am very fascinated with faeries. Frankly, I'm excited you popped into my window!" She clapped her hands together and grinned at the faeries. "Perhaps I could be of assistance?"

The faeries exchanged glances wordlessly.

The mint-haired faerie spoke up again. "You see, there is a thief that has been stealing our wings. The thief knows where we reside, gets past our magic defenses, and rips the wings right off of us!" The mint-haired faerie crossed her arms and huffed in frustration.

The woman's face morphed into a look of concern. "That's horrible. How would they know where you are? It's very difficult to find faeries!"

"That's the tricky part. We believe the thief was once a faerie that a wizard turned into a human long ago, therefore they have the long life of a faerie, possess the capabilities to track us, and can withstand our magical fortifications."

"That is very tricky indeed, and quite interesting." The woman said, now deep in thought, long fingers twisting her dark locks absentmindedly.

"Do you think you could help us turn them back into a faerie?" inquired the smallest faerie in a squeaky voice.

"I certainly think I could!" the woman asserted "I have studied faeries for years. Like I said, I find your kind quite fascinating, and so beautiful." She flashed them a warm smile. "I have a tome here somewhere that spoke of this legend and how it could be done!" The woman started sifting through her books, tossing some safely out of the way onto a plush velvet window nook.

The faeries shared looks, understanding without words what they needed to ask. "What form of payment would you require for your services?" the faerie with the midnight hair asked.

The woman looked up from her search. "Payment? Hmm. Would you visit me sometime? I would love to have faerie friends!" She beamed at them, her violet eyes crinkled with pure joy.

The faeries collectively let out a sigh of relief. It was not often a human was so kind to them. Faeries tended to keep to themselves and their domain. But, kindness goes a long way.

"I would love to!" The smallest faerie squeaked and flew around the woman's head, twisting into her hair.

The woman giggled, her face lit up with happiness. "My name is Asgurn! Oh, I found it, here we go!"

She hefted a dusty tome and set it on her wooden table, flipping to the required page.

"Here!" She pointed to a spell listing what was required to transform a faerie into a human. She scratched her head in thought as the faeries gathered around the page.

"This doesn't explain how to change them back though, does it?" inquired the mint-haired faerie.

Asgurn nodded. "I have an idea: we can utilize reversal magic with the spell. I think it would work like a charm!"

Asgurn was clearly an intelligent and well-versed witch, not to mention radiated with kindness. The faeries trusted her.

She winked at the faeries. "Now, how do we find this thief?"

Many of the faeries waited in hiding up in the trees. Asgurn, using her invisibility spell, was hiding down in the brush outside of the faerie runes so as not to trigger their painful effects. Asgurn had met with the faeries, including the Head Faerie, and was briefed on where the defenses were, the plan, and what the thief looked like as far as what the faeries had glimpsed. Asgurn was kind, adored the faeries, and all the faeries had taken quite a liking to her.

They had been in this position for the last three days, taking small breaks to eat and rest, waiting for the thief to return. They were all ready for action the moment the thief showed themself. The traps were set, and one brave faerie took on the role of bait. A faerie with lavender hair and plush lips lay peacefully on a flower, her body stretched across the petals and her wings flapping gently with the breeze, the beautiful colors catching the sun's light.

A twig cracked.

Every faerie in waiting and Asgurn tensed, and shortly the thief appeared, shrouded in dark clothing. The thief silently approached the faerie on the flower, who played her role exquisitely, pretending not to notice as the thief got closer. Suddenly, roots sprang up from the ground and entangled the thief, pulling so tight they couldn't move. Asgurn appeared from the brush, waving off her invisibility spell and quickly reciting the reversal spell's words. Her dark hair whipped around her face, her violet eyes glowing with power.

The thief turned their head towards the witch but made no sounds, as if they were accepting their fate.

Six faeries gathered above the thief, flying in circles and sprinkling magic down upon them. Asgurn continued with the spell, and soon a bright, shimmering magic enveloped the thief. As it grew brighter, the witch nodded at the faeries above the thief to back off so they would not be harmed. She drew closer, chanting louder. With a bright flash and fizzling *pops*, the magic dispersed and only glimmers remained. As those faded away, a small faerie sat in the place the thief once was.

The small faerie had crimson hair and deep brown eyes. Asgurn drew nearer and knelt beside the now-faerie once more.

"Hello, little thief."

She smirked at the faerie, and the faerie returned her gaze. Those brown eyes began to well up into tears. Soon, the faerie was sobbing, its fiery wings drooping. Asgurn scooped up the faerie in her delicate hands and carried the wailing faerie to the rest of the stunned gathering.

"Isalyn?" The Head Faerie flew through the crowd and knelt next to the crimson faerie.

"Father?" she asked between ragged breaths, tears streaming down her face.

"I knew you loved that human... I had an inkling it could have been you, but why Isalyn? Why would you do this to your kin?" The Head Faerie's face showed a mix of agony and relief, tears now spilling down his cheeks.

"I... I don't know. It has been so long. So long I have been alone and my love long lost. I didn't know what to do, and I had to survive. I missed my wings, all those beautiful wings..."

The Head Faerie gathered Isalyn in his arms. "Well, you are home now, my dear. But your misdeeds cannot go on unpunished. We had decided ahead of time, if this plan worked, what must be done."

Isalyn looked up into her father's eyes with deep sadness and yearning. "Do what must be done."

Squeaky, that was her nickname now, had gone to stay with Asgurn for a while to help her learn, and they had become dear friends. Plus, she did not want to see when the faeries ripped off Isalyn's wings. It would be painful, dreadfully painful, because it wouldn't be one quick pull by a giant human, but an agonizingly slow tear done by many faeries. But they would grow back. Probably.

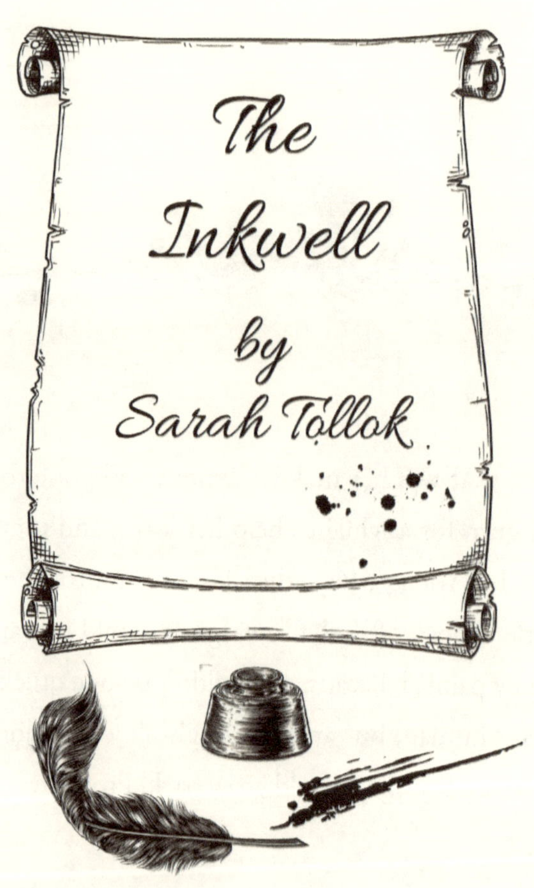
The
Inkwell
by
Sarah Tollok

Sarah turned around twice, slowly, not knowing where to begin. Working in a public library with its industrial metal stacks didn't compare to the perfectness of this space and its floor-to-ceiling built-in shelves, each filled to the brim with vintage books. She would have liked nothing more than to curl up in one of the comfy chairs, light a fire in the grate, and start making her way through reading the collection one by one.

Then, there it was.

It was every book lover's dream...the rolling ladder. She stifled a giggle as she gripped the brass rails, climbed up to the second step and gave it a good push. She glided only about four feet before the wheel snagged on the edge of a rug and stopped abruptly, sending Sarah's face into the handrail. At least she didn't break her glasses; she couldn't afford a new pair.

She could have sworn she heard a faint chuckle. Was there someone else in the mansion working on clearing out some other rooms? The pale, little estate lawyer with thinning hair and a permanent scowl she had met earlier implied she was the only one in the house that day.

"I'm not sure what the library director told you, but the estate of Mr. Byrne has been through a series of court disputes over this past year since his death. With matters finally settled, I am able to release the itemized portions of the will. Actually, what you're here for has never been in contention. I guess no one found they had use for these books," he explained as he opened the double doors to the gorgeous room.

Upon entering, she spent a moment gaping at the rows and rows of books, the stained glass above the window seat, the fireplace, the plush velvet reading chairs, and the beautiful writing desk. That morning, when Sarah had been tasked with boxing up and transporting some donations, she had inwardly groaned about it, expecting a shelves of dusty, outdated encyclopedias, mold-ridden Reader's Digests, or crumbling National Geographics. But this? Oh, she could live out her years in this room and be quite content.

The lawyer huffed and looked at his watch, bringing Sarah back to her senses. She did some quick calculations, estimating how many books she could fit into each box and compared that to how many shelves lined the room.

"This collection is amazing! I brought the library's van and lots of boxes, but I'm not confident I could get this all done in one day." Sarah reported with what she hoped was an apologetic smile.

"It's the furniture as well," the lawyer replied in a brusk tone followed by a long sigh.

"Didn't your director give you any details? The will specifically stated that the Byrne Regional Library was to receive 'the entire contents of Mr. Byrne's personal library.' Considering that the late Mr. Byrne founded and endowed the library, one would think they would have anticipated the extent of this collection."

"Receiving such a generous gift is unusual for us. Most people just drop off boxes themselves. We, of course, wanted to handle such a special donation with a personal touch. I'll take the utmost care of Mr. Byrne's books and other items. I just don't think I can fit it all in the vehicle I brought with me today."

"Well, do as much as you can. If we must make an appointment for another day to finish up, I suppose I can have my assistant come out and unlock the house for you. I'll leave you to it until this afternoon, when I come back to lock up. There is a dumbwaiter just past the next door, if that can be of help to you getting the boxes downstairs. The powder room, should you need it, is in the front hall. There should be no reason to enter any of the other rooms."

He gave her a pinched smile and then was off.

Sarah dabbed at her swollen lip with a napkin from her lunch box, a half-moon of blood staining the paper from where her tooth cut into her lip upon impact. Sighing, she straightened her glasses, picked up her bruised ego, and got to work. As she carefully transferred the books to the boxes, it was hard to resist the urge to flip through the pages, check the copyright dates, and see if there were any interesting inscriptions.

Maybe she'd see some of them again at the next Friends of the Library Association semi-annual used book sale. Getting early access before the sale officially opened was a job perk Sarah never missed the opportunity to take full advantage of. She pushed away the thought of the overflowing bookshelves in her little apartment and the fact that her to-be-read pile was already unrealistically ambitious.

Sarah was very grateful for the working electric dumbwaiter, but she still needed to take a breather about two hours in. Her thighs were starting to protest against more trips up and down the stairs, and the dust was getting to her. She called her boss to give an update and discussed making arrangements to get the heavy desk, the chairs, the grandfather clock, and all the knick-knacks out of the library and to the auction house. He asked Sarah to clean out the drawers of the desk to prepare for its eventual removal.

After hanging up, she grabbed an empty box and started through the desk. She found a lovely fountain pen set, some vellum stationery yellowed with age, a pretty glass paperweight, a few pairs of old wire-rimmed reading glasses, and a wax seal kit on its own silver tray, complete with several sticks of wax in various colors. Everything but the old paper, destined for the bin, went into the box. Since it wasn't full yet, she placed it on the window seat until she found more knick-knacks to fill it.

Just as she was about to close up the desk and move on, something struck Sarah as being off. Looking back and forth between the two open drawers, she realized both were pulled out as far as they would go, but one was much deeper than the other. She pulled at the shorter one, thinking it was just stuck, but it held fast. Shrugging, she made to close the drawer, but a wayward piece of vellum paper floated off the desk and slid to the back of the drawer.

She looked over her shoulder at the stained glass window. She hadn't felt a draft, but there must have been one coming in through somewhere. When Sarah reached to grab the paper, her finger slid over a little indentation near the back. She ran her finger over it again, then pressed. There was a definitive *click*, and the drawer shifted forward a touch.

Sarah pulled the drawer again, and this time it slid out easily. Built into the back of the drawer was a box with a small keyhole in the top and a ring to pull it open. Sarah's imagination supplied her with so many possibilities about what secrets it held. An antique pearl-handled revolver to ward off would be book thieves? Cash and bond notes worth millions? Perhaps love letters from some clandestine affair?

Sarah pulled the ring, but the lock held strong. Her shoulders slumped. Her little treasure-hunting adventure appeared to have come to a premature end. She thought about how if this took place in a mystery novel, there would have been someone around who was handy with an improvised lock pick. But Sarah was not one of those nimble-fingered characters.

She returned to packing books and thought about how it was probably best that there wasn't a way for her to get at the contents, anyway. She had student loans to pay off for that BA in English Lit, and her car probably wasn't going to pass its next inspection. Savings? Nil. She loved her job as a library assistant because she got to be around books all day, but it didn't pay well. So, if there was some precious treasure that no one knew about but her, it would have created a moral dilemma.

She packed books, books, and more books. During her lunch break, Sarah settled into the cozy window seat and tried not to spill her cold cup of vegetable soup as she scrolled through the bookish side of social media on her phone. Thanks to the bright midday fall sun filtering in through the stained glass, it was a toasty spot in the otherwise chilly house. Just as she was reaching for her bruised pear, Sarah smelled something vaguely familiar that was not food. She closed her lunch box and sniffed. A candle? But she hadn't lit any candles, nor were there any in the library that she had seen.

"Oh! The sealing wax!" she exclaimed out loud, reaching for the box of desk items she had placed at the other end of the window seat.

Sure enough, the sticks of sealing wax had been sitting in the sunlight long enough to start to melt, looking more like sad crayons than the rectangular sticks they were when she lifted them from the desk drawer. She moved the whole box to the floor and surveyed the damage. She prodded the one that looked the worst to see just how soft it had become. Something poked her finger. There was something small and hard in the stick of wax. Sarah leaned in closer, carefully separated the soft wax, and discovered a delicate silver key.

"No way!" She said to the empty room.

The grandfather clock on the other side of the room rang once, making Sarah jump. The relic ticked a few times, then fell silent again. Sarah sat down hard in the desk chair and laughed out loud.

"Well, that was dramatic timing!" she said to the clock, then laughed some more about the fact that she had been packing books in silence for so long, she just talked to a clock.

She turned the key around and around between her fingers. Finally, she shrugged her shoulders, pulled out the drawer, and plunged the key into the lock. It fit perfectly and turned smoothly. She pulled the ring, and the door popped open, soft as a sigh.

At first, Sarah wasn't quite sure what she had found. There were a few long feathers at the back of the compartment and a small clay vessel with a matching lid. She lifted it out and opened it, then peered inside. Liquid? She sniffed it.

"Ink?" she queried to no one at all.

"Yes, of course it's ink. What else would you find in an inkwell?" Responded a voice from behind her.

Sarah yelped, dropped the lid, and spun around to find an elderly man sitting on the window seat she had perched on only moments ago. He was holding her brown pear. She made some more nonverbal noises of surprise as she instinctively clambered up on top of the desk.

"Where the hell did you come from?" She finally yelled when she was looming above the stranger.

"The short answer - we came from the inkwell you are holding. Which, by the way, be mindful not to spill please. It will stain the lovely mahogany of the desk." At this, he paused his assessment of her fruit and tossed her the lid. It must have been from pure adrenaline that Sarah, usually not the most coordinated, caught it with her free hand.

The old man pantomimed putting the lid on the jar. Dumbstruck, but never one to risk damaging an antique, Sarah capped the jar.

Seemingly satisfied, the man continued, "The long answer: we arose from the desert, long before the children of Allah and Yahweh came to be and made war with one another. We also came from a little coal mining town in central Pennsylvania, the son of poor Irish immigrants who were beholden to the company store from the moment their father stepped foot in the mines."

It was on the tip of her tongue to ask what the man meant by "we", but then she stopped short. She noticed they spoke in two voices at once. And their eyes! With each blink, two different personalities shown through. One of them burned hot with an ancient fire and leapt with excitement. The other was kind enough, but also tired. If someone had asked Sarah how she understood this duality, she would have been completely unable to explain it.

"What year is it and who are you?" The two-person man asked.

As they lifted the pear to their mouth and took a large, slurping bite, Sarah noticed their hands were delicate but dexterous and covered with age spots. They closed their eyes as they waited for the answer, savoring the taste and not at all unnerved by the young woman standing on top of the desk, clutching a weighty hunk of pottery in her hand like a baseball pitcher mid-pitch.

Sarah was too baffled to come up with any other question or response besides the plain truth.

"It's 2022. My name is Sarah. I work for Byrne Regional Library as a library assistant. I'm here to empty out this room. It was willed to the library by the owner of the house."

The being's eyes shot open at her answer.

"2022?! Why did it take so damn long? Oh, let me guess, my darling great nieces and nephews tried to contest things. Ungrateful brats! Well into their 60s and still acting like foolish children."

When they spoke that time, it was just the old man, Sarah was sure of it. It was like he stepped further into the spotlight and took over. That's when she recognized him. She had passed his portrait a dozen or so times every day at work. It was the same man who had owned the home, and who had founded her library. He was the dead man whose will she was there to carry out the wishes of.

"You're not a ghost. I mean, you're eating my pear. But you also aren't just Mr. Byrne either."

"Quite right, clever girl. We are still partly Charles Byrne, but we are not completely alive, nor are we dead. Additionally, we are something else entirely. We are older than you can comprehend. We have lived many different lives over, and yet we are always the same. We are very powerful, and yet we are imprisoned. We are Jinn."

Sarah looked at the coupled personalities in front of her. They gazed back at her placidly, as if allowing her time to process everything. Then she turned to the jar—the inkwell—in her hand. She rubbed her finger along the rough surface, felt the lines of wedge-shaped writing along the curve of the side. It fell into place in her brain, made oddly perfect sense, as fantastic as it all was.

"So, you're saying you're a genie," she held the inkwell in front of her, "and this is your bottle."

The jinn smiled and gave Sarah a little nod. They then picked two tissues from a nearby dusty dispenser on the desk, wiped off their sticky fingers, wrapped up the pear core and perfectly pitched it into the wastepaper basket on the other side of the room without looking.

"Now that we understand one another, would you like to get down off the desk?" They offered her a hand.

The hand was solid and warm. It was a normal hand. Sarah stifled a nervous laugh at the ridiculousness of being helped off a desk by a genie, err, *jinn*. The jinn took a seat in the desk chair as Sarah moved back to the window seat. She was about to ask a question when the jinn cut her off.

"Yes, we will grant you a wish, but it is only one wish, not the three that is so often falsely advertised. So choose wisely. I cannot stress this enough...*choose very wisely*. Once you write your wish with the ink in that pot, you are bound to living out your wish."

Sarah would have made a nerdy reference to that scene with the Templar Knight from *Indiana Jones and the Last Crusade* if the circumstances had been different. But both the jinn and the old man—Mr. Byrne—were so gravely serious in their warning that Sarah could do nothing but swallow heavily and nod in agreement.

As the jinn continued, their voice became something deeper, richer and more powerful; something laced with magic and mischief but also touched by melancholy.

"We can make someone think and act like they love you, but we cannot make them truly love you. We can kill your enemies, entire armies even. We can bring you great wealth, power, or even immortality. But you must then live with the consequences of that wish. If you summon me to revoke the wish, then you will share my prison with me until another makes a new wish."

"That's how…" Sarah gestured at the old man-shaped entity before her.

"Yes," the old man's tinny voice took to the forefront again, "We…I found the inkwell hidden in the house of one of the coal barons. I was only ten years old, but I was already working as a breaker boy, picking slate out of the coal, for almost a year. My father was a miner, and my older brother was a mule boy, pushing carts to the breakers. My mother was a housekeeper for the mine owner.

"It was Easter Sunday and the mine was closed. They didn't give her the day off, though. Told her to do some deep cleaning and change the drapes out when they were away visiting family. So, she took us all to the big house with her to help out.

"It was nice and warm in there, nothing like the company house we lived in. She gave us all baths in the big tub. I wandered off and poked around where I wasn't supposed to be. There was a big grandfather clock, and I was mystified by it. I opened it up to see all the gears, and I found the inkwell hidden inside. My wish was to provide for everything my family needed or wanted."

"I mean, that's not a bad wish, right? It clearly worked out okay for you." Sarah swept her arms around, indicating the house and all that it held.

"At first, it was wonderful. I lifted my family out of poverty. My father, already sick with the beginnings of black lung, had the best doctors that money could buy and outlived all his old friends from the mines. Mother never had to wash other people's laundry again, nor did she have to cry over a poor crop of beets and potatoes from our little patch of garden, knowing that it would mean a lean winter and more debt at the company store. She was able to pay a maid to wash our clothes and a cook to make a Sunday roast for us every week, although she still insisted on doing all the baking herself.

"My brother and I got to go to school, and even college. My little sister was born after I made the wish. She never knew about going to bed hungry and cold. Seeing her grow up without all those worries was wonderful. And I admit I spoiled her and my own children rotten. But each generation that I provided for grew more and more dependent upon what was handed to them.

"The money just kept showing up in their bank accounts, without anyone having to do anything for it. They had all that they 'needed and wanted', but it only ever led to more want. And they also kept procreating. As long as

I had more and more family to provide for, I was trapped; old but never dying. All the people I truly cared for were long gone. The money wasn't doing anyone any good anymore, because it was all they ever knew.

"So I took it back. My body died, my spirit is here, and the money flow dried up. That's why they all fought so hard about the will."

"Except the books," Sarah reminded him.

"Except the books," Mr. Byrne responded with a smile. "Founding the library was one thing I never regretted. Since I couldn't provide them with a yearly stipend anymore, this final donation was the least I could do."

"You didn't think anyone in your family would snoop around in here? Find the inkwell?"

"The one thing I learned about people who have grown up very rich is that they have no sense of curiosity. And I was right! And here you are."

"Wait," Sarah said, her face scrunched up as it always did when she had to do mental math, "The library was founded in 1910, and you died in 2020. No one ever questioned why you were around for that long? Or where all the money came from?"

They chuckled, a deep sound that started in their chest and bubbled out. Then they leaned in close to Sarah, said in a stage whisper, "You and your co-workers never questioned how I could have started the library in 1910 and yet I still attended the fundraising gala every year for over one hundred years, did you? Magic, dear girl, remember?"

They leaned back in the desk chair, fitting into it perfectly. Sarah was reminded that it was their chair, after all, and their library that she was sitting in.

"So, you took your wish back, and…"

"Then I," the voice shifted back to its dual nature once again, "became 'we'. But once you make your wish, the soul once known as Charles Byrne will be freed completely to the ether of time."

The expression that accompanied this was both content and lonely all at the same time. Sarah wasn't sure which emotion belonged to which half of them.

"Wow. This is, like, A LOT. From what you told me, and from all the sci-fi I've read over the years, I am guessing that great big repercussions could come from seemingly totally benevolent wishes. I mean, money can corrupt. And asking for world peace could maybe erase whole cultures. Or even wishing for the cure for cancer could, I don't know, make a huge population explosion or allow someone to live who was supposed to die but now they are going to be the next Hitler or something."

The jinn nodded sagely and appeared to be amused by Sarah's thought process.

"I don't think I could wish anyone dead. And again, repercussions and ripples in the pond and all that. I've never been one for romance, so wishes related to love don't hold any appeal for me."

"And we can only make someone appear to love you," reminded the jinn.

"Yeah, that's nonconsensual and creepy as hell." Sarah said, her face twisted in disgust.

The jinn's face matched hers. "None of my kind like doing it. It feels worse than murder. Usually, people at least had a decent reason for using their wish to want someone dead."

It was then Sarah's turn to nod. Before continuing, she asked, "I'm sorry, what do I call you?"

"Charles would work fine. Or Charlie. That's what my mother always called me. Our other name is not conceivable to mortal minds."

"I'd rather you don't blow my mind any more than all of this is already, so, Charlie it is," Sarah smiled and sat down, but then the weight of everything hit her in another wave.

"My life is very different now than it was just fifteen minutes ago. I have the world at my fingertips."

She put her head in her hands and just took deep breaths for several long minutes. Charlie waited patiently and silently, watching the fall leaves blow around outside through one of the clear panes of glass.

"Okay," she said finally, getting down to business, "So, really big wishes are probably too dangerous. Maybe I need to think smaller, and about what brings me happiness. I could wish myself out of debt, but that seems like a waste. I'll pay off my student loans and stuff, eventually. I could go on a dream vacation but, again, that seems too trivial. I'm only twenty-five, so I have plenty of time to travel. And, truth be told, when I'm on vacation I mostly just like to find quiet, beautiful places to read so..."

Sarah gasped and put her hand to her mouth, then gasped again.

"Oh my god, I think I know...but how would that work? I mean, there's only so much time. But it really is my fondest wish, always has been."

Sarah started to pace around the library as she spoke, running her fingers over the spines of the volumes she didn't get around to packing yet. Then she turned back to Charlie, squinted, and asked, "Am I allowed to ask you about what other people wished for in the past and how it turned out for them? Or do you have some jinn code of confidentiality or something, like doctors and HIPAA?"

"We don't know who this 'Hi-pah' is that you speak of. We are happy to tell you about the wishes of others. Ask away."

Sarah took another deep breath then asked, "Has anyone ever made a wish about wanting to read all the books?"

"Yes," Charlie replied with a wisp of a wry smile.

"And how did that go for them?" Sarah asked, eager and wide-eyed.

"They revoked their wish one hundred and eighty-seven years later. All their family were dead and gone. They read many things they loved and some things that were awful and horrific. They read day after day, decades on end. The wish provided for their basic needs to be met and for their life to be extended until the wish was totally fulfilled. The wish granted them access to every book. As soon as one was finished, another one appeared. There were textbooks, holy books, great works of fiction and some tirades of hate. There was romance, physics, cookbooks, poetry, diaries, and instruction manuals.

"They wanted to be done, but they had wished to read 'all the books that ever existed and those yet to come'. The only way out was to revoke the wish. They enjoyed the quietude of the inkwell with me for many years. They told me their favorite tales, and I was happy to listen. They were released from their bond with me when a little boy found the inkwell and wished that his old dog could run again and live as long as he did. That wish, it should be mentioned, was never revoked."

"That was a damn good wish. The dog one, I mean," Sarah replied.

"Yes. Yes, it was," Charlie agreed. "The dog's name was Sasha."

"Is it common to word wishes poorly and not get the results one was looking for?"

Charlie pursed their lips as if to stifle a laugh. "It...has happened, yes."

"Okay, you can't make that face and then not tell me the story behind it."

The jinn sat up straighter, said with a mock formal tone, "It is not just one story. There have been several, umm, gentlemen who have wished for a certain part of their body to be larger. They have not always specified how much larger, or what they mean by the subjective term 'huge', or that it was to be an augmentation of their current equipment, as opposed to an additional, new, large, umm..., and where that new item should go on their body."

"Charlie!" Sarah squealed. "You scoundrel! You have the wisdom of centuries of existence and decided to play dumb about THAT? Oh, my god! How many times did that happen?"

"Seven," was their quick response.

"SEVEN?!" Sarah yelled, dissolving into laughter.

When the last of the laughing fit passed, the gravity of her situation settled in her bones once again. She sat on the opposite side of the window seat from Charlie, brought her knees up and hugged them like she did when she was little and had big questions to ponder. When she went to rest her head on her hands, she winced back. Her sore lip had landed on her knuckle in just the wrong way.

Charlie made a chiding *tsk-tsk* noise, then flicked their fingers in her direction. Sarah's lip tingled. When she touched it, it was completely fine, no more cut or swelling.

"Thanks!" she said, then, "Woah, I didn't wish for you to do that, so..."

Charlie waved away her concern. "Don't worry, that one was for free."

He picked up a book and started leafing through it with fondness.

"Charlie—I mean, other part of Charlie that isn't Charlie—can I use my wish to free you?"

They looked up at her with wide-eyed surprise, which quickly spread into a wide, warm smile.

"Dear girl, you are so kind to ask! No, you can't free me. It actually takes two jinn, both simultaneously receiving wishes to free the other. As you can imagine, simply getting two jinn in the same place at the same time is extremely difficult. It's an entirely other matter to find two people who are willing to both give such altruistic wishes."

"Oh, I'm sorry."

"Don't be. We appreciate you asking! Most don't. But let's get back to your wish about reading. We feel it has real merit."

"Why are you helping me figure this out? I mean, you gave seven guys mutant members over the years, so why be so kind to me?" Sarah asked, daring to look Charlie straight in those mesmerizing eyes of theirs.

"You, Sarah of the Byrne Regional Public Library, are a book person. Book people tend to be good people. Reading makes their hearts more compassionate. We've been all around the world, and this almost always holds true. And from what we've seen from you so far, you are definitely one of those good book people."

Sarah blushed at what was possibly the best compliment she ever received in her life. She felt ready to get back to the business at hand.

"Okay. So, the other reader you talked about made the mistake in the wording of it. They said they wanted to 'read all the books'. Therefore, they were obligated to continue to read until they read all the books, right?"

"Correct, Sarah."

She got up and started pacing again. "So it would be better to wish for the ability to read all the books, because that doesn't obligate me to do so, but would give me the option to. But how would that work? There's still only so much time in a day and in a lifetime. I don't want to be immortal. That would probably eventually suck."

Charlie raised their grey, shaggy, old-man eyebrows and gave a noncommittal nod. Then they craned their neck to peer into Sarah's open lunch box.

"My dear, do you happen to have any chocolate? If so, could I trouble you for some?"

"What? Oh sure, side pocket. I grabbed a handful of Halloween candy from a bowl in the break room the other day."

She watched Charlie struggle with the plastic wrapper for a moment, then finally get it right. He sniffed at it deeply before taking a nibble. It was so ... human.

"Charlie, when I make my wish, then you'll, like, die?"

After allowing the last taste of chocolate to melt on their tongue, Charlie eventually replied, "The man known as Charles Byrne will be released from this union. He was able to take care of his loving parents, and his wealth did do some good in the world, like your beautiful library. And he has tasted chocolate one last time. He is ready and at peace. Now, kind girl, we will give you a hint."

The jinn beckoned Sarah closer. She wasn't sure why this show of conspiratorial whispering was necessary, as they were completely alone in the big house, but she rolled with it.

"We can bend time. We can also create pockets in time, where one can go whenever they want, and do whatever they want. Then, when they are done doing whatever they want, such as reading a book, they can exit that pocket of no-time and resume their normal lives."

Sarah understood. She was quiet for several minutes working it out in her head. Then she stood and straightened her cardigan. She retrieved the inkwell from the desk. Charlie stood up in kind and faced her.

"Charlie," Sarah said through unexpected tears rolling from her eyes, "I know what I want to wish for."

Charlie produced a monogrammed handkerchief from their pocket, gingerly wiped the traces of chocolate from the corners of their mouth. They snapped their fingers and a scroll appeared on the desk. He plucked a pair of reading glasses from the nearby box and donned them on the end of his nose. They fit perfectly. Charlie unrolled the scroll to a new, unmarked section. Peeking out from the section above was a name, "*Charles Byrne.*" It was not in the showy script that one would have expected from the rich man who had a library named after him. It was the careful block lettering of a little boy with limited schooling.

Sarah ran her fingers over it, whispered, "You were so little."

Charlie gently took the inkwell from Sarah's hand and removed the lid. He retrieved one of the quills from the open desk drawer, dipped it, and handed it to Sarah.

"Are you sure?" She asked one more time.

Charlie nodded. "Thanks for the chocolate, and for giving my story a good ending. Happy reading, Sarah."

The quill was satisfyingly scritchy as Sarah wrote, "I wish for the ability to step out of time when I am reading, and then for time to resume normally from that exact moment again when I am done reading."

Charlie bent over the desk and blew on the ink to dry it. Their breath smelled of desert sand and exotic spices, then changed into the scent of old books and new books, of leather and ink. Charlie's exhale lasted for what seemed like ages. Then, they rolled up the scroll and looked Sarah deep in her eyes.

"Granted."

A great light grew within Charlie until it was so bright that the form of Charles Byrne could no longer be seen. Sarah could have sworn that just before he vanished completely, he winked at her. Then, there was only the power of the jinn. It was almost unbearably bright, although it was somehow made of both fantastic light and deep darkness. It was chaos and harmony. It was too much. Sarah felt spun and lifted and like she was falling, all at once.

When Sarah came to, she was curled up in the pillows of the window seat. She was waking up from what felt like the most satisfying nap of her entire life. She heard the grandfather clock ticking. Had it been ticking all day and she just now noticed? Was that what woke her from her nap? She had been dreaming, she was sure of it. The dream was fantastic, and it smelled like spices and chocolate.

"Ms. Hudson! Is the library paying you to sleep on the job?!"

Sarah shot to her feet and nearly knocked over a nearby box of desk supplies in the process. The lawyer had returned and was several shades redder than his earlier pale complexion. As he berated her and threatened to call her supervisor, Sarah tried to clear her head and orient herself. She improvised an apology and let him know her boss was already making arrangements for the removal of the furniture and that yes, she would be happy to return on whatever day his assistant was available to allow her back in to get the rest of the books. Appeased, he told her to grab whatever last box or two she could carry and he would meet her out front to make sure things were locked up properly. He did not offer to help her carry anything out.

When he left the library, Sarah hurried to gather her personal items and close up the last two boxes. As she was about to close her lunch box, she noticed empty candy wrappers inside, as well as a handkerchief. There in the corner, ornately embroidered, were the initials C.B.

Sarah ran her fingers over the letters, whispering, "Thank you, Charlie."

She then picked up the nearest book, took a seat, and began to read. The ticking of the clock stopped. She read page after page. As she was flipping from the first chapter to the second, she glanced out a window. The falling leaves hovered in mid-air. Sarah went back to reading.

Don't Step in
Fairy Rings
by
Marie C. Erikson

I spent the weekend trapped in the fey realm, but I managed to not be late for work on Monday morning. It was what my mother would call a photo finish: staggering in through the front door at 8am with my hair pulled up in a bun to hide the fact it was still wet.

I hadn't had the energy to shower the night before. I'd stumbled back into this plane of existence on Sunday evening, surprised to find my car was still in the parking lot where I'd left it. I'd driven home, found that my house key still worked and collapsed into bed. The next morning, I'd woken up sweaty and panicking with barely enough time to shower and dash off to work. Once I made it there, the hard part was figuring out what to do next.

I sat down at my desk and stared at the cubicle wall. I'd forgotten how things could be so flat and beige. My head was spinning. I remembered it was safe to eat and drink things here and went to the break room to get some coffee.

Danni came by while I was starting the coffee. "Leah, did you party too hard last night?" She laughed at herself, though she hadn't said anything funny.

"No, the fairies got me." I put a filter in the coffee pot, but couldn't remember how much coffee I was supposed to use. I opened the canister and stared at the little scoop inside. The coffee smell was stronger than I remembered.

"Did you step in one of those fairy rings? You know you're not supposed to do that." Danni didn't even seem to be doing anything in the break room, just staring at me. She would probably ask even more questions if she saw me reading the instructions on the back of the coffee canister.

"I know I'm not supposed to do that." I just dumped coffee in until the filter was about half full and hoped that would work.

"And if you do end up in the fey realm, you're not supposed to eat anything or give out your real name or make deals."

"I didn't," I said. "I followed all the rules." Now I had to wait for the coffee to brew. I turned away from her to look for a mug, hoping she would take the hint.

"If you did everything you were supposed to do, then you should have been able to get out quickly. That's how it works."

I didn't say anything, just got a mug from the cupboard and set it down next to the coffee pot. The refrigerator had a bottle of vanilla caramel creamer that hadn't expired yet, so I grabbed that too. I didn't realize how tense my shoulders were until I felt them relax after Danni left.

I tried to actually get some work done once I had coffee, but had to ask IT to reset my computer password. Years had passed while I was inside the fey realm and I couldn't remember my password, even though it was only two days on the outside.

Cole came by to check on me while I was in the process of remembering how to do my job. "Is that the coffee from the break room?" he asked. "I don't know who made it today, but it's way too strong."

Apparently, I'd promised Cole last week that I would send him some information he needed first thing this morning for a report that was due by the end of the day. I had no memory of that conversation, but it sounded like something I would do.

"I'm sorry," I said. "I'm still trying to remember how to do everything."

"What happened?"

"Fairies." I stared at my computer screen, hoping he wouldn't press the issue.

"Did you make some kind of deal with them and it backfired?" His voice sounded worried.

"No, I got pulled into the fey realm and I spent a long time trying to escape. I never made any deals." I really did not want to have this conversation.

"The fey aren't that bad. They usually let you go pretty quickly, unless you piss them off or agree to something you shouldn't."

"They tortured me." It was difficult, but I managed to keep my voice neutral.

"The fey don't torture people. That's not something that happens." He sounded genuinely confused, like he was trying to figure out how I'd misunderstood everything.

I promised to send Cole the information by lunchtime, and that satisfied him enough that he left me alone.

I was on my third cup of coffee and halfway through getting the information together for Cole when I saw the pixie under my desk. My hands started shaking when I saw her, and the coffee cup slipped through my fingers as she started flying toward my face, hitting the carpet with a dull thud.

"What do you want?" I yelled. I realized people could probably hear me, but I didn't care. "I left. You're not supposed to follow me here." Not that anything else had happened the way it's supposed to happen.

The pixie was maybe a foot tall. Like the other pixies I'd seen, she looked pretty from a distance but scary up close. Her skin and hair were a shiny silver hue, with teal-colored wings that looked like dragonfly wings. She also had very sharp teeth and a necklace made out of bones. "I didn't follow you on purpose," she said. "I got pulled through the fairy ring when you left and now, I'm stuck here. I need you to help me get back."

"Nobody helped me," I snapped.

I tried to ignore her, but she hovered in the air around me, flapping her wings.

"My name is Kina," she said. "You're Leah, right?"

I tried to focus on soaking up the coffee with paper towels.

"I should at least give you my name, because I'm depending on you to help me right now."

"Is that actually your real name?"

"Yes. I know yours, so it's only fair."

I threw the wad of paper towels in the trash can. "Your people don't normally just give out their names like that." I didn't know if I could believe her, but I felt too burned out to care. "I don't know how to help you, I'm sorry."

I managed to get the information that Cole needed to him before lunch. Kina got bored hovering around me and started playing with things on my desk. I watched out of the corner of my eye as she figured out how the stapler worked, then tried to figure out how to use the staple remover. She seemed to have the right idea, but her hands weren't large enough to maneuver it.

Cold iron was supposed to work against fairies, right? I wondered if there was anything made of cold iron inside the office.

I got lunch from a taco place down the street and ate it in my car. I didn't think I could stand being around people while I was eating. I tried to eat slowly and remember the names of all the different flavors in the food, but it was hard to focus on anything when I felt numb and hyper-vigilant at the same time.

Kina was still there when I got back to my desk. She'd made a little chainmail coat for herself out of paper clips, and she was trying to use the computer.

"How do you use this?" she said. "I saw you typing words earlier, but I can only make stars."

I watched as she pressed random keys in the field where I was supposed to enter my password. She'd apparently been doing this for a while, because an error message came up that I was locked out of my account for too many tries. I sighed as I called IT to ask them to reset my password again.

I spent most of the afternoon staring at the computer and trying to force myself to do something. I knew I would just be behind tomorrow, but it was really hard to make myself care. I vaguely remembered that I used to enjoy my job.

Kina was still playing with things when I left for the day and I assumed she would stay at my desk overnight, or at least that she would stay until she had played with everything there. I didn't realize she'd stowed away in my car until I was a block away from my house. When I saw her, I panicked again and stopped the car abruptly in the middle of the street. Another car honked loudly as it swerved around me.

"Sorry!" I yelled to no one in particular. "I'm sorry," I said again.

A second car changed lanes at the last minute to avoid hitting me.

My roommate Bethany was waiting for me when I got home. "Where were you?" she asked. "And what's that?"

"I was at work? Also, this is a pixie who's been following me." Kina's paper clip chainmail made a jingling noise as she waved at Bethany.

"No, you were gone all weekend. You usually tell me if you're going to be away. I was worried about you."

I'd been planning to sit on the couch and relax for a while, but I suddenly wanted to escape to my room. "The fairies got me," I said. "That's where she came from. You wouldn't know how to help her get back, would you?"

"Don't you know better than to mess with fairies?" Bethany looked shocked, and Kina flew around the room as if to demonstrate how dangerous she was.

"I didn't do it on purpose. I must have stepped in a fairy ring while I was taking a walk in the park." I had been trying to get more fresh air and exercise lately. I didn't think I would ever take a walk again after everything that had happened.

"You shouldn't step in fairy rings. I thought everyone knew that. Didn't your parents teach you when you were younger?"

I turned and walked down the hall toward my room.

"She needs to help with bills if she stays here more than a few days," Bethany said.

I was too jittery from all the coffee to sleep, but I was too exhausted to focus on doing anything. I ended up lying in bed and staring at the ceiling. The caffeine had probably been making me freak out a lot more than normal, too. I felt stupid for not realizing that earlier.

"I don't know how to help you," I said to Kina. "I don't know why you're still following me."

"You could at least try to step in the ring and open the gate between our worlds?" She made it sound like the most simple and obvious thing in the world.

"I don't even want to get close to the ring. What if the same thing happens and I get stuck there again? I can't go through another round." I could feel my whole body tensing up just from thinking about it.

"You keep saying you didn't like it there, right? How do you think I feel?"

"I don't know." It's not like anyone was torturing her.

"Time moves faster there. My wife has probably been looking for me for a long time." I could hear her hovering in the air somewhere behind me. The clinking of the paper clips was getting annoying. "I'm so small and weak here, I hate it. Everything feels wrong."

"Yeah, I know what that's like." I was still facing the wall, but I knew she could hear me. "I didn't have anyone to help me, but I didn't go around nagging people. I spent a long time trying to get out on my own." I almost felt bad for her, but it wasn't my responsibility to help her. I did *actually* feel bad for her, the more I thought about it. Everything in this world probably felt as wrong and un-natural for her as the fey realm had for me, and it wasn't her fault she was trapped here. It still wasn't my responsibility, though.

Kina flew over to the side of the bed so that she was in front of me. I sighed and rolled onto my stomach, burying my face in the pillow.

"Why are you so worried about possibly going back to the fey realm?" she asked, because apparently nobody in my life could read body language and take a hint. "You don't exactly seem happy here, and you just argue with everybody you meet."

I lifted my head to look at her incredulously. "Nobody believes me!" I was snapping at her, louder than I'd intended, but I didn't really care. "That's my problem. My life was fine until I got trapped over there and went through hell and now nobody believes me."

She flew back around to the other side of the bed and sat down cross-legged on the pillow. She wasn't jingling around and playing with things anymore, she was just watching me. "What exactly happened to you?" she asked.

I took a deep breath. "I realized where I was and I tried to remember everything I'd been told. I actually tried to look it up on my phone, but I didn't get any service in the fey realm. I remembered, though. Don't eat anything, don't give your real name, don't make deals. Don't be too confident or too scared, because that will just draw attention to you. Just keep your head down and look for ways out, and especially don't try to outsmart or out-trick the fey. I did all of that, but it didn't do any good. I still couldn't find a way out."

"You said you were there for years. Did you go that long without eating anything?"

"Eventually, I started feeling faint from not eating and at that point, I had been there for so long I figured not eating wasn't helping me. Maybe I should have held out longer, I don't know. It didn't matter because I was captured by one of the fey courts."

"Which one was it?"

"I don't know. I don't think they ever told us their name, and I'm not sure I could have pronounced it, anyway. There were a bunch of humans there and they kept all of us in cages when they weren't doing things to us. They did... experiments. That's what they called it, anyway. They took the air out of my lungs, suffocating me but never letting me pass out, spending hours choking on nothing and struggling to breathe. They hung me upside down in midair and turned my eyeballs around backwards and dropped me down a tunnel or something, falling forever but never hitting the ground. I don't even remember all of it, but it was horrible. When they weren't running experiments on our bodies, they used us as game pieces. We were all set up on a field and they told us where to stand- I think they were playing Go? There was also a game that reminded me of Risk, where we had to fight each other when one player wanted to take over another player's territory. Eventually, another fey court showed up and fought with them and they let all of us go. They said we could leave, but I couldn't find my way out. I kept looking. I never saw any of the other humans again, so I think they managed to escape, but I spent at least another month just looking for an exit."

I felt raw inside after saying everything out loud. I waited for Kina to respond, for her to tell me that it shouldn't have happened or that I just should have done things differently.

Kina was silent again before she finally spoke. "For what it's worth, I believe you. Everything that happened to you was horrible. You didn't deserve it, and it shouldn't have happened. It wasn't your fault."

I broke down crying. It was ugly and pathetic and as quiet as possible because I didn't want to deal with Bethany knocking on my door and asking if I was okay. I lay there in bed, curled into myself tightly and sobbed until my nose was running. I sat up to look for a tissue or something to blow my nose, but couldn't find anything. I ended up wiping my nose on the sleeve of my shirt. I'd been planning on washing it, anyway.

I noticed movement out of the corner of my eye. Kina was slowly walking toward me on the bed, like she didn't want to startle me. I suddenly felt huge and disgusting next to her. She wrapped her tiny arms around one of mine to hug me.

"I'm sorry," she said. I tried to respond, but I just started crying again.

"Fine, I'll try to help you," I said once I was able to speak coherently. "But not until tomorrow, when it's light outside. I need your word you'll help me get back here if I cross through. I don't want to get trapped again."

"That's fair. I promise that if we cross back over together, I will do whatever I can to help you come back here." She spoke in such a serious voice I was inclined to believe her. I knew fairies don't make promises lightly, but I also knew that they like to exploit loopholes to trick people.

I called in sick to work the next day. We drove back to the park, and I found a parking space that wasn't far from the trail where I'd passed through the fairy ring before. I felt shaky being back there, and it felt as if time had slowed down even more. Kina squeezed my arm again.

The trail disappeared into the woods, but the place where I'd gone off the path wasn't too far away. I found the creek I'd left the trail to look at. It was just a normal creek with rocks and flowing water; pretty but definitely not worth everything that had happened.

This time, I saw the ring of mushrooms in the grass. Kina hovered in the air above the ring.

"You tried going back through here yourself?" I asked.

"Yes. It doesn't work for me on this side." To demon-strate, she lowered herself to the ground and stomped her feet on the grass inside the ring, but nothing happened. I assumed it had to be like my futile efforts to cross back over from the other side.

Kina flew back up to me and sat on my shoulder as I stepped inside the ring, on purpose this time.

It was instantaneous. I had the feeling of falling for a moment. Then, the air pressure changed, and I was back in the fey realm. Just the smell of it made me feel terrified and sick to my stomach.

Kina was next to me now, and *growing*. She grew larger until she was the size of a short human. She still had sil-ver skin and teal-colored wings, but she was wearing a lot more jewelry now and I could tell she was powerful just by looking at her.

"That's a relief," she said. "I was worried my body would never go back to normal."

I turned around and tried to look for the portal again, but of course, there was nothing. I berated myself for being stupid enough to trust Kina when I heard a voice.

"You're okay! I can't believe you're back!"

It was one of the leaders of the fey that had rescued me. I'm pretty sure she was an archfey? I didn't remember her name or her exact title, but I knew she was important. She and Kina hugged tightly and kissed each other. I thought about how the wife of royalty had been following me around and playing with my stapler, and I almost forgot to be afraid.

"I remember you," said Kina's wife. "You were one of the prisoners, right? I can't believe you came back here willingly. What can I do to repay you?"

"I want to leave," I said immediately. "I want to go back to the mortal realm, where I came through." I worried that I still wasn't being specific enough and she would find some way to twist my words.

"I can open a portal for you, but I owe you a favor if you're ever back here. I hope you know I don't say things like this lightly."

She drew a circle in the air with her fingertip and I could see trees on the other side of it. They were normal-looking trees, not the weird fey plants.

"Thank you," I said as I stepped through it. I could hear Kina saying goodbye to me, but I didn't want to risk turning around and missing my chance to leave.

I stumbled through the portal and collapsed onto the ground. Everything felt surreal, though I'd been here only a few minutes ago. I crawled away from the fairy ring as quickly as I could and ended up lying on my back in the grass.

It was actually kind of relaxing, lying on the grass and looking up at the sky with the sound of the creek running next to me. I lay there for a few minutes until I could convince myself that this wasn't a trick.

It occurred to me the weather was nice, and I had the rest of the day off work. Nothing felt normal or even okay and I didn't know when it would again, but felt like I could at least finish the walk I'd been taking the other day. I got up to my feet and started walking.

The Honey Tree

by
Jay Levy

Part 1 – The Pool Party

Swimming at Annabel's house was the best. Well, second best if Abigail also counted spending time in the sun. Which she absolutely did. She was an Elf of the Sun, after all.

Anna was Abbi's cousin. They were about the same age and had close to the same features: thin, young girls with pale skin and sparkling blue eyes. Anna's hair was as dark as the ocean's depths, but Abbi's was yellow as the golden sun. They were often mistaken for sisters, something they both enjoyed.

While the pair lived close enough for frequent visits, Anna was close to the shore, and Abbi wasn't. If she could, Anna would spend all her time in the water, whether it was the backyard pool, the ocean, or the bathtub. She was quite the little mermaid, literally.

"It's warm and delicious out here." Abbi turned over on her pool side chair to let the sun heat her back.

Abbi's mother had never cared about sunblock. Not that it mattered. She could spend the entire day in the sun and not feel its burn. But come nightfall, Abbi's skin would radiate heat that slowly emanated until the sun rose again. It was said that Elves of the Sun once lived alongside the ancient tribes of men. The Elves sat as open-air hearths for tribes of wandering humans at night, who, before recorded time, set up their tents and basked in the elves' heat for comfort, light, and wisdom. Enough Elves of the Sun could warm a city all night, but their numbers had grown scarce in the ravages of time. City elves were even fewer these days.

"You daydreaming?" Anna splashed Abbi from the pool, while Evelyn, Anna's mermaid friend, swam up to them both, rising out of the water with her clamshell bra and wet, flowing red hair. Abbi feigned anger, but then smiled brightly at the pair and splashed them in return from the side of the pool.

Evelyn was Anna's companion: an ageless friend that hid as a small doll in plain sight when those who couldn't understand magic were around. It wasn't only adults, but anyone who didn't care for the workings of magic in daily life. While the doll could be removed from the house, Evelyn couldn't show herself outside of the home. Unlike Anna, Evelyn never went without her tail and her need to be in water was constant when she wasn't masquerading as the doll.

Anna's in-ground pool took up most of the backyard, leaving only a few feet of grass around the outside of the cement pool deck. A six-foot tall wooden fence with two gates boxed in Anna's backyard, adding protection against outside sounds. The first at the shallow end opened to the driveway. The second at the deep end led out to the woods behind Anna's house. That one stayed closed and was mostly ignored by the girls. What lay directly behind her house was a lush copse of trees, and behind that, a noisy shopping center.

Evelyn turned to Anna suddenly.

"Someone's coming," she said and dove under the water, circling Anna from below the surface. Evelyn knew everything that went on in and around the house. Somehow, she sensed when people were coming and going, fighting, sleeping, and everything in-between.

The driveway-side gate opened, and a pair of strangers—a man and a woman—stepped through.

Evelyn emerged from the water and cleared the hair from her face. "Ernest, is that really you?"

"Hello, lovely Eve." The man stepped forward and bowed. He wore a flamboyant shirt akin to a disco ball, which bounced the light in glaring patches. The reflections would've blinded most, but not Abbi. "Lovely to see a familiar face... and tail." He winked, and Evelyn blushed.

Ernest was a tall, thin man with blonde hair, blue eyes and pointed ears, just like Abbi. He seemed familiar, but she doubted ever seeing him before. Other than his reflective shirt, Ernest wore dark slacks, boots, and a jacket that looked stolen off the set of a pirate movie. It was no wonder why Evelyn was fond of him; he looked the part of a modern swashbuckler—complete with guy-liner, five-o'clock shadow, shoulder-length hair, and rapier at his side.

Standing behind Ernest was a muscular, homely woman, about six feet tall with broad shoulders. She had a large, beak-like nose, black straw-like hair which hung past her shoulders, and massive teeth in a square jaw. Her loose denim jacket stopped just above her waist, her black boots were royally scuffed, and she carried a thin, black club tied to her belt.

"You haven't changed a bit, have you, luv?" Ernest said, only looking at the mermaid. "You're still as beautiful as I remember."

Evelyn's blush intensified. "I know. I'm sorry it's not the same for you."

He bowed again. "It's true. Aging affects me as any other mortal." He stroked his gray-streaked goatee, as if lost in thought. "I've gotten older and I have the laugh lines to prove a life well lived. It's been years since you saw me, and since I've seen you girls." He nodded to Anna and Abbi.

"You know us?" Anna asked from Evelyn's side.

Ernest nodded. "I'm not surprised you don't remember. You would have been... two, maybe three, at the time."

Evelyn splashed Ernest playfully with her tail. "Speaking of remembering... how about that one night, with the sailor, you, me, and the boat, the last time I saw the ocean? We need to make memories like that again and soon."

Ernest laughed, but he blushed this time.

Anna looked at Abbi and mouthed the word 'ocean' with raised eyebrows.

Suddenly, the tall, square shouldered lady cut into the conversation. "Where are your mothers?"

Abbi and Anna looked at each other, but it was Abbi who spoke. "Mom's inside."

"Girls?" A woman's voice, Abbi's mom, spoke from inside the house through the cracked open patio door. "You alright out there?"

"Yeah, Momma," Abbi called back over her shoulder. "We're all ok out here. Just chatting."

"You girls holler if you need anything. Okay?"

"Yes, Mama," Abbi answered and repositioned in her chair. "Mama's just inside," she continued quietly to Ernest and the other woman. "While we're out here, we have Evelyn. She protects us." Abbi pointed to the mermaid, who expertly splashed water in the direction of the two visitors.

"I could think of better things for that tail, luv," Ernest blew the mermaid a kiss.

Evelyn smiled, her face reddening, and she dove under the water.

"Look girls," he continued, "my friend here's just trying to be helpful."

"I didn't mean anything by asking..." The tall girl stomped and folded her arms.

"Truth is," Ernest said, "Mags is not much older than you two. But you'd never know by looking at her."

"Oh, perfect, thanks!" Mags' voice dripped with sarcasm and she growled. It was more primal than a young woman should sound. "Thanks for blurting out my business to them."

"I thought maybe since they were close to your age..." Ernest closed his eyes and shook his head. "Regardless, it's the truth. She's my student, and a half-troll, rare in these times."

Mags grumbled something about trust and ground her boots into the pool deck's cement.

A half-troll, Abbi realized, would explain the girl's height and build, even if she originally figured the girl was an adult. However, now that she knew, Abbi noticed the teenage girl, just like herself, hidden behind the massive muscles and square jaw.

"Mags, huh?" Anna said. "What's that short for, anyway?"

"Maggot."

"Oh," Anna blushed. "That's your name? Really?"

Ernest smirked. "I keep telling her, Maggie, Margaret, or Marguerite would do better than Maggot. But this is the name she keeps."

"I like Maggie," Anna smiled.

"I do, too," Evelyn said.

"But, my name is Maggot." The tall girl's jaw tightened and she looked away.

After an uncomfortable silence, Evelyn broke the ice again. "So, what business brings you here after all this time? I assume it isn't a social visit. If it was, you'd have been here a long time ago."

"Ouch," Anna smirked in Ernest's direction.

"You're right." He rolled his head on his shoulders and clasped his hands together to keep them from shaking with anxiousness. "It's not just a coincidence. I know what lies beyond that gate at the deep end of your pool. I've come to make an appeal." He cleared his throat. "I beseech your permission to journey past the gate in search of the mythical syrup. Annabel, Keeper of the Gate of the Southern Honey Tree, I—We," he motioned between him and Maggot, "we need the honey from the tree and its properties. Please, will you help us?"

Anna looked over to Abbi, who shrugged. "What did he say?"

"He wants us to open the gate so he can go get honey from the tree."

"Oh. Sure," Anna smiled. "Why didn't you just say so?"

"It's that easy, then?" Mags asked. "You're just going to let us?"

"Yeah, of course." Anna shrugged. "I only keep the gate safe. I don't bar anyone from entry. If people want to try to get honey, that's their own business. It's dangerous, you know."

Anna climbed out of the pool and as she left the water, her legs returned mystically, as if her mermaid side had never been present. Abbi saw the change every time and knew to look for it. No doubt Mags and Ernest noticed too; such things were commonplace to those in the know.

Abbi followed behind Anna and watched her open the fence's gate, revealing trees and bushes behind. Evelyn swam to the deep end and jumped out onto the side, but kept her tail in the water. She looked like a calendar pin-up girl, the way she leaned back on her arms, the water glistening off her wet hair and shell-bikini, but Abbi knew Evelyn only wanted to be as close to her charge as possible.

"Dangerous you say? Not to worry, we can handle ourselves." Ernest motioned to the blade at his belt and tapped

Mags' belly. "This girl's wearing chainmail and has a special magic club given to her by a wizard. And I'm one heck of a swordsman."

"I'll say." Evelyn blew him another kiss.

The gate opening ritual was one Abbi had seen many times. It always reminded her of cutting a pizza, the way Anna sliced the open air, touching all the sides and corners of the open gate. At the end of the last slice, her cousin paused, finger hovering over the middle connection point of all the slices.

"Before I complete this ritual, I must speak these words..." Anna took a deep breath and spoke what Abbi had heard numerous times before. "Stepping within is done of your own free will. The path ahead is lit by the sun, and the point is the point."

"What does that mean?" Mags asked. Annoyance tinged her voice.

Anna shrugged. "I don't know."

"We've never been on the other side," Abbi added.

"Never?" Ernest failed to hide his surprise.

Both girls shook their heads.

"Gathering the honey comes with risk," Anna said, "but the reward is great."

"Indeed," Ernest stroked his chin stubble. "Come, Mags, let's not dally longer."

Mags nodded and cracked her knuckles.

"It only stays open a second and you get one shot," Anna looked to Mags. "When ready to come back, do as I did on that side. Make the motions and be sure you tell it you're ready to hop through. We may not have ever traveled to the other side, but we do know the way to get home."

Anna flicked the middle of the gate and it fell inward in eight separate slices, like a gust of wind pushing through a broken mirror. It revealed swirling blue and purple lights funneling inward like a whirlpool. The air should've been displaced by the movement, but all was inexplicably still.

Abbi smiled when Anna stood aside and the strange duo leaped into the swirling blue gateway like so many had before.

Part 2 – The Honey Tree

Maggot fell hard when she jumped through the gate. Having chainmail under her sweatshirt didn't help the impact, but it was a good thing that she went through first. Ernest fell right on top of her and she broke his fall. Thankfully, he was light. If she had landed on him, she would've broken something on the slender elf.

Not that Ernest was weak, but he wasn't half troll.

Maggot helped her friend to his feet and looked around, not knowing what to make of things. They were no longer in a beachside town. The smell of salt in the air was gone, as was the immediate stench of chlorine from the girl's backyard pool. Now, Mags was standing on a well-packed dirt road, surrounded by trees.

She squinted and looked both ways. "Looks like this road leads nowhere in either direction. Where the hell are we? My head's spinning." She leaned over against a tree and vomited, hating every moment of her vulnerability.

"How can we be in the middle of a forest now?" She wiped the remnants of their last meal off her chin. Unable to hide the hesitation in her voice, she didn't even try.

"It'll be ok, Mags," Ernest's tone was calm, "like we practiced. Five simple breaths, in and out."

"I'm not angry..." she shook her head. "Just confused."

"We passed through a gateway. The displacement is normal, designed to make us feel like crap once we've passed through. We aren't on Earth anymore. It's another realm."

Mags stood solemn for a few moments. Her eyes closed, she breathed deeply, and Ernest laid a hand on her shoulder. The gesture was appreciated. She wasn't comfortable with enough people to want any kind of physical touch... other than at the end of her knuckles.

"The girl," Ernest said, "told us the path will be 'lit by the sun.' What do you think she meant?"

Soothed, Mags looked in both directions and pointed. "We take the path under the shining sun."

Ernest nodded. "I agree. Ahead we stride. You ready?"

"Almost," she ripped off a piece of her sleeve and tied it around a small branch. "So we know where we can leave."

"Good thinking." Ernest patted her on the shoulder again before they walked away.

After several minutes, Mags couldn't help but complain, albeit in the form of an understated observation.

"This forest is vast," she said.

"In truth, we can't see deep into these woods," Ernest countered. "For all we know, the ocean, or some other body of water, is on the other side of those trees, just out of sight."

Mags stopped and listened. "No, if there was, we'd smell the ocean or hear the waves. I've lived near water long enough to know when it's close."

Ernest shrugged, ending the conversation.

The duo traveled until they reached a fork in the road, which diverged into identical looking paths half the size of the original, with neither beneath the glowing sun. A skeleton of a very large man sat propped up against a tree at the fork.

"He's not a Troll." Maggot nodded to the leaning skeleton. "No burial weapon or armor."

"How do you know it was a 'he,' hmm?" Ernest winked. "Could have been a she. Must've had clothes once, shame none remain. Funny, even though the bones are brittle and sun bleached, they're still in their proper places." Ernest beckoned for Mags to follow and bent closer to examine its ribcage. "Come here and look at this thing."

"Could have been a Giant." Mags kept back, keeping an eye on the path. "Maybe standing a dozen feet high or more."

"Huzzah!"

She turned to see Ernest stabbing the tree behind the deceased giant's rib cage.

"I've pierced you through the heart, foul creature, and now you die!" Ernest laughed loudly and looked behind at Mags with a large grin.

"Cut that out." She eyed the path. "You're dishonoring the dead."

"It's only in jest." He pulled his blade from the tree and sheathed it. "I'm sure this dead giant doesn't mind, or know. Besides, when will I get the chance to stab a giant through the heart and survive?"

She rolled her eyes. "The girl said 'the point is the point.' What point?"

Ernest examined the skeleton.

"Perhaps this, here. Come closer?" he beckoned for her again, and this time she complied. "Look, a finger is extended on that hand. It must be 'the point,' right?"

"I suppose," Mags agreed, and they went the way the skeleton suggested. It led them to a clearing, one with a large tree as a focal point in the dead center. The tree oozed an amber, sap-like fluid from its cracked bark.

"Honey," Mags sniffed the air. "I can smell it from here. Smells so very sweet." Abnormally large wildflowers bloomed brightly in the clearing before them. Bees the size of coconuts flew about the blossoms like striped farmers, collecting pollen, rushing this way and that, before delivering their bounty.

"Not to mention what it's supposed to do… fight disease and addiction, heal and nurture the sick, perhaps even stop death…"

Mags raised an eyebrow at her friend's colorful description. He was, after all, on this mission due to a hunch—all to save a dying man, an elder of his kind and mentor he couldn't bear to lose. As Ernest's student, it was her duty to follow his lead and help, even if others thought his quest a fool's errand.

Here they were, in front of the legendary Honey Tree. If what Ernest said was true, then she was glad to have been wrong.

"This tree holds vast secrets and power." Ernest grinned.

"There's far too much bee activity," Mags pointed to the swarm in the flower field.

"Use caution when crossing," Ernest advised. "Let's not upset them, shall we?"

Quietly, they started through the field. After a few steps, Mags stepped on something brittle and it crunched underfoot. She looked down to see what it was.

Bones lie strewn about, resting undignified against weapons and in armor, entwined within the roots of the weeds, brush, and flowers that buried them. Legacies of failed adventurous types who'd come here and died.

A skull rolled next to Mags's foot and she jumped. It rumbled, the jaw opened and out flew a bee, buzzing into the air.

Ernest laughed, more than he should have.

"It's not that funny," Mags said through clenched teeth.

"It is from where I'm standing. Don't worry; I won't let the jumping skulls get you." Ernest picked up the skull and held it so he could look into the empty sockets. "Be still, old warrior. I honor thee." Ernest's eyes glowed for a moment, bright and white like the Sun. "May the glories of the Sun give you warmth in the ever after and allow you peace in your rest."

The skull crumbled into dust in Ernest's hands. Gently, it flew upwards towards the brightly shining Sun, sparkling as if the dust might carry more than bone.

"You haven't done that rite in a while." Mags didn't want to add that, most often, Ernest was too drunk to care about 'nonsense' such as old rituals and honoring the dead.

"It felt right, somehow." Ernest shrugged.

"Shame you can't honor them all."

"True," Ernest picked up another skull, one with large tusks jutting from its lower jaw. "It was part of what we, Elves of the Sun, did for creatures in ages past. Helped them move on. But there are so many here..."

Mags followed his gaze across the field. Everything she had thought was a rock could turn out to be bone.

"However," Ernest's moment of introspection seemed over with a smile and a grin. He pointed at the tree, and posed with his foot up on a log, in his 'captain-stance' as he called it. Catching the sunlight, his shirt reflected light patches around this field of forgotten souls. "We have a goal! Let us not forget our reason for being here."

Mags smirked when a large bee flew past Ernest's head, forcing him to duck. His stance of personified leadership shifted promptly to cowering behind Mags.

"It'll be alright," she mocked his earlier tone. "I won't let the big, scary bees get ya." This time, Mags laughed.

Ernest harrumphed, and the pair approached the tree. The bees' buzzing and movements intensified.

"I'm not sure about this..." Mags said when they'd approached close enough to touch the tree.

Ernest caressed the bark, rubbing his hands up and down the trunk, ignoring the large bees crawling around. He giggled and slapped it, causing little droplets of sap-like honey to fly off. Several bees jumped from the honey laden bark and hovered about the pair, just out of arm's reach.

"Yes!" he hollered, "We made it! Let's get our bounty and get out of here!"

Tree-crawling bees vibrated and buzzed more intensely, their abdomens shaking with aggression. Some exposed their stingers. Others from inside larger holes in the trunk flew out and started buzzing in a swarm around the tree's crown.

"I don't like this," Mags said. "Stop what you're doing! It's pissing them off."

"Anna warned of the danger," Ernest smirked, "but we've faced *dozens* of hazards, and survived. We got this, luv! You have the bags, right?"

Mags pulled a bag from her back pocket. It looked like a deflated volleyball with a rigid plastic straw jutting from the top.

"Excellent," the elf continued with excitement, "get to work. I'll distract the bees." He patted Mags' shoulder, stood, and spread his arms before walking away. "Come get me, you rowdy little bastards..."

At about ten paces away, his skin illuminated, radiating bright sunlight. His heat was immediate and threatening.

The bees felt it, too, and those on the tree flew toward Ernest, as he ran around the field. Mags could only watch for a few moments as his glowing body leaped over bones and logs, weaving this way and that, zigzagging patterns in her vision.

Mags knew better than to stare, but forgot this time. After a few moments of blinking away the spots, she got to work using a hefty-sized screwdriver to punch holes into the trunk. With a solid thud, the tool forced its way through the woody meat to the honey behind. She then inserted the straw part of the bag into the puncture. Honey drained faster than anticipated, and the bag started to fill. Mags quickly punched two more holes, festooning each with another straw and bag, and then stood guard as the honey flowed.

But the bees knew what she was doing. Once she'd punctured the tree three times, the insects reacted. They dove from the tree's crown, wings humming.

She heard them and dodged their dive bomb attacks, internally chastising herself for forgetting to bring something that smoked to help calm the anxious bees. She could smell their airborne pheromones mixing with the wildflower aromas in a heady perfume. It was doubtful Ernest noticed. While he had many gifts, superior smell was not one of them. She could tell by their scent, the bees were angry.

Several more charged Mags, darting at her in quick succession. This time, however, she fought back with the screwdriver and split a few down the middle. Their severed bodies flew away in goopy messes, falling among the skulls and bones of the dead.

Mags dodged and ran as more bees followed in close pursuit. One flew past her head, almost impaling her cheek with an eagle's claw-sized stinger. It buzzed loudly, distracting her, and she fell when her foot caught on the skull of a long forgotten warrior. The skull crunched and Mags' heart sank. She landed on the ground, twisting to fall on her back, but knocked the wind from her chest.

A bee landed on her chest. Its mandibles glistened with saliva, its eyes jiggled, and its antenna twirled aggressively before her eyes.

But a rock, flung from somewhere off to her side, hit the bee and sent it flying away.

Ernest's heat got closer, and with it, her friend and mentor.

"Now, now, no lying down on the job!" He bounced past as quickly as a flash of light, laughing as he pulled along his own swarm. "Quickly... maneuver nine."

Ernest pulled the gathered swarm along, the bee's deafening buzz reminiscent of an eighteen-wheeled truck barreling down the highway. He looked like time-lapse photography—a blurred line running in a circle around the field, with the condensed swarm on his heels.

Mags wasted no time. In a single motion, she pocketed the screwdriver and unlatched the leather strap holding the sleek, slim, and black club at her side. Her finger itched against the button at the bottom of the handle, just waiting for the right moment to press it.

Ernest's circle was almost completed; she could see the reflecting light beaming from his disco shirt. Right before he reached her, Ernest tucked and rolled. Mags pressed the button and roared. She swung in a wide, infinity loop pattern and the club came alive, blooming with an electric glow and arcs of light tracing her movements.

Some bees escaped, but many did not. They crashed headlong into the wide arcs, fried into smoking husks, and tumbled to the earth below. Those she hit with the club itself exploded—covering her in gooey blood and chunks of fuzzy carapace.

Once the baton's flash stopped, the much-reduced swarm retreated.

"Ha!" Ernest called out. "We're victorious! I knew maneuver nine would work."

Mags frowned as she plucked bee parts from the wiring of the club. "My weapon helped. Although I don't understand how it works...," she shrugged. "I'm glad the batteries didn't give out. Not sure they could do it again."

"No matter, get the bags so we can get out of here." Ernest pointed with a nod of his chin. "They're regrouping above the trees. See?"

Mags couldn't look, but hurried, plucking the bags from the trunk and capping the straw-like tops. She gave each a squeeze. Two were full, one was half full; it would have to do.

"Let's go." Mags ran past Ernest, hopping over bones and smoldering bees.

He didn't answer, but she heard his steps following hers, just like she heard the buzzing leave the treetops to come after them.

Sweat beaded on her brow, but Mags dared not look back, lest she lose her nerve and her lead.

Ahead lay the threshold between pathway and tree's clearing. If only she could get there...

"Close your eyes." Ernest's voice was gentle and calm. Mags knew what was about to happen next would be anything but.

Behind them, Ernest flared.

She saw the light before hearing the sound of his voice, and instinct told her not to look back at her friend, not even a brief glance over the shoulder. When he flashed like this, Mags knew the light could sear your eyeballs from within.

The bees, however, didn't. They were looking right at Ernest as they came up behind, and Mags pitied them. Flames kissed the back of her neck, giving her a sunburn feeling, and her backside was singed.

Ernest was giving it everything he had left.

Finally, Mags jumped from the clearing to the path, landing in the dirt with the bags held close to her chest. She rolled to a stop, got to her knees, and tested her sight before fully opening her eyes.

There was no more flash, just Ernest standing above her with his hand outstretched.

"Come, my friend," he said, helping her to her feet, "why lie in the dirt when we have an objective looming? No time to dally."

"But..." Mags pulled the club from her belt and looked around, expecting bees to swarm at any moment. They didn't.

At the threshold between the path and the clearing of the honey tree, two bees hovered—big, fat, fuzzy bumble-bee types. The other chasing bees had apparently turned tail and retreated.

But these two... they glared at Ernest and Mags.

"They look angry," she said, shifting the bags of honey on her belt uncomfortably. She moved side to side and the bees followed her every sway. "That's creepy. I'm getting out of here."

"Right behind you," Ernest laughed as they both turned and walked away from the buzzing bees.

The walk back was quiet... except for Ernest's gloating about the worst part of this adventure being over. Mags wondered if the bees' stingers would have penetrated her chainmail shirt, but couldn't get a word in edgewise.

"I get it!" Mags threw her hands up, frustrated. "You kicked ass and saved our butts. Only I'm the one covered in bee guts."

Ernest tried to hold back laughter, but couldn't. "You rhymed. Did you know that? Butts and guts?"

At that point, it was contagious and the tall half-troll joined him in a raucous roar.

At the fork in the road, they paused again at the giant skeleton sitting against the tree.

"That poor fellow," Ernest nodded with his head. "He just sits there all day, no one remembering him, no one paying him any visits. Forgotten. Lost..."

"Occasionally stabbed through the heart by glory-hungry idiots." Mags countered as she started walking again, brushing past her mentor.

"*Touché.*"

As Mags got a few dozen paces away, Ernest said, "oh, I see, you beat me to it. Sometimes I forget you can be as devious as me."

"What're you going on about now?" She turned around, returning to his side.

"Oh, and coy, too. I like this new Maggot. Did you dip into that honey and it gave you a big set of balls or something?" He mimicked a monkey carrying a couple of coconuts between its legs.

"Balls?" Mags stared at Ernest with wide eyes when he waddled as if carrying heavy objects below his crotch. "What are you talking about?"

"The skeleton." He pointed with a nod. "The hand. Great idea. Not sure when you had time to get to it, but glad you did."

Mags pushed past the elf and looked. Both the skeleton's hands were closed.

"No one passing by will get the clue of the 'point.' Brilliant, Mags."

"I didn't touch the skeleton. Are you kidding me?" She crossed herself in a very human gesture. "I'm not into those kinds of bad vibes. I disturb the dead as little as possible."

"If not you," fear touched his voice, "then..."

A moan cut Ernest off, low, stagnant, and deep. The skeleton's mouth dropped open.

Mags jumped back. "Did you hear that?"

"It's the wind," Ernest assured, but couldn't hide his fear. "Let's move on, shall we?"

But in front of them, small pricks of light lit deep in the skull's eye sockets... and the mouth closed.

"Run." Ernest dashed past Mags, quicker than she expected. She wasn't prepared, though instinct chided that she should have been.

With a shriek, the skeleton rose, stepped forward, and swiped at Mags in one fluid motion with claws of rough bone. In her moment of hesitation, it connected and Mags screamed. Bits of metal ripped from her chainmail and blood sprayed from her chest.

"Ernest..." she called out and tried to fall to a knee. But the skeleton wouldn't let her.

With a large, round-house punch, the skeleton hit her again, sending her backward like a fast-moving tumbleweed.

"I got you." Ernest was suddenly at her side, helping her to her feet.

"I'm hurt."

"I know." His eyes turned gold, and his skin heated. He reached forward and laid a hand on her chest, searing the flesh of the wound. "Forgive my touch."

Ernest gritted his teeth and pushed heat into Mags' chest; she felt stronger with the warmth encircling her heart, but rage boiled.

The giant skeleton bounded near, and Mags gasped at its sudden approach. With a single leap, it was suddenly behind her mentor and, with both hands, raked a vicious attack.

Blood cascaded outward in arcs from the elf's back and he spun, removing his healing touch. The monster grabbed Ernest's shoulder, but he twisted away, stumbled several paces aside, and collapsed. The golden glow in his eyes and the heat escaping his skin stopped. Ernest gasped for breath, and then closed his eyes.

"No!" Mags hollered. She unlatched, grabbed, and swung the club from her belt in one fluid motion. Jumping, she connected with the giant's skull and spun it in place; the skeleton floundered back several steps.

"Pick on someone your own size!" Anger saturated her words, the pain in her chest forgotten. "I can best a moldy, old set of bones." Her finger hovered over the club's button.

The skeleton's skull spun around and it stood tall, revealing its massive, fifteen-foot stature. Then, it tilted its head, reminding Mags of a Rottweiler wondering what to do with a small, yipping Chihuahua. It lunged forward and swung a massive bone claw, but Mags countered with the club. She hit the button at the last moment, filling it with a crackle of electricity. The skeleton and the club connected with a clash of shattering energy, and the skeletal monster pulled away. Its pinprick eyes focused on the club dancing with electric fire.

The skeleton shrieked again, but Mags heard something in it she hadn't before—hesitation, fear.

She couldn't let it distract her, not now. The skeleton swung again and she ducked, spinning and tumbling under its body. From behind, she swung the club with both hands at its femur. When the club connected, the bone cracked from top to bottom, and the skeletal monster roared, louder than before. It was loud enough to hurt Mags' ears.

Quicker than she expected, the skeleton pivoted its weight and spun. She swung again, but the monster grabbed her club hand with its left hand, and her neck with the other.

"Own size..." it repeated, whispering like a breeze through gravestones.

The skeleton crushed both her hand and the club in its massive grip. Electricity crackled when the club shattered and she screamed as the surge flowed through her arm, burning her fingers. The skeleton then head-butted her in the face, and she saw stars in swirling colors. Finished with her for the moment, it tossed Mags aside like a broken toy.

Thankfully, when the colors stopped dancing before her eyes, she saw the skeleton was concerned over its leg.

"It's hurt," Ernest said weakly at Mags's side. She hadn't heard him approach, and was thankful he was conscious. Even injured, he moved as silently as petals in the breeze. "We need to go, now."

"I can't feel my hand." Mags's eyes filled with tears, but she dared not let a drop spill.

Ernest nodded, took hold of her, and led them both further down the road. She could feel whatever heat he had left running into her hand, but it didn't help much.

Behind them, the skeleton shrieked and hobbled after. Its one leg seemed as stiff as a board, and the monster, ill-prepared to move with such an injury.

"It's just down the road a spell," Ernest consoled with a smile.

Mags didn't feel like chiding him for cracking a joke at a time like this.

Turning back towards the skeleton, Ernest called out to the monster. His voice was smooth, like golden honey on a bright, sun-filled day.

Mags knew this trick—he let the light and warmth of the sun into his voice, and tried to sway the creature, to calm it, even to force it away... but nothing. Either the skeleton was too stupid to be impressed by Ernest, or it didn't care.

Either wasn't good, and the skeleton kept approaching.

"We need to flee." The words felt strange as they left Mags' mouth, each syllable betraying a little more fear. She grabbed Ernest and pulled him along. He dragged his feet, locked in his attempt to beguile the skeleton. His attempts stopped once it ripped a tree from the ground, pivoted, and hurled the freshly uprooted javelin into the air like a lawn dart.

When it landed near the pair, dirt exploded around them in a shower of forest floor debris. They looked at each other with wordless alarm and hurried to the gateway location as fast as their injuries would allow.

Another roar from the skeletal monster preceded another tree ripped from the ground.

"Hurry now..." Ernest pleaded. He meant to be tough in the moment of panic and fear, but Mags knew him too well. Not even the Sun in the sky could calm his panic at this moment. "You have to do it. Just as the girl said."

Finding the cloth she tied, Mags started tracing the lines in the air like Anna had; her mouth dried, and her mind blanked.

Next to them, a tree crashed into the ground, closer than the last. It caused them to stumble and interrupted Mags' placement of the lines in the gate; her only choice was to start again.

"It's ripped up another tree!" Ernest gritted his teeth. "Mags, hurry! I think it's ready to throw..."

She couldn't focus on Ernest, the skeleton, or trees, and drew the last remaining lines in the air.

"We want to go..." she whispered to the gateway as she touched the center.

Another huge tree crashed into the ground.

Part 3 – The Escape

On the pool deck closest to the deep end, Abbi lay flat on her stomach on a towel and continued enjoying the brightness of the sun. Then, to her surprise, the gateway opened.

"Anna, look!" She shouted.

"No way!" Anna swam over with Evelyn close behind. "They made it back?"

When the misty, blue swirling light suddenly appeared, Abbi expected the tall, buff girl and the smarmy pirate Elf to come stepping through.

Only tree branches emerged.

After a second, the gateway closed and the branches were instantly cut off, as if by the sharpest blade. They fell onto the deck and some into the pool.

"What a mess." Anna pointed to the branches. "Who's going to clean this up?"

"I wonder why branches?" Abbi said. "Where's Ernest and Maggot?"

Anna shrugged. "I guess the same place the rest go when they don't come back."

Abbi sighed. "I wanted to ask him about when we were little. I got the photo albums from inside and everything."

"I would've liked to see Ernest again, too." Evelyn pouted from the water, longing in her eyes as she looked at the gate. "It's a shame you girls can't go in after them."

"You know we're only allowed to open it on this side one time for each person. Rules are rules. The gate would break if we tried." Anna sighed and looked at Abbi. "I guess our questions will have to wait for another time."

"If ever..." Abbi shrugged. The weight of the many who'd never returned hung heavy on her shoulders, and she could only imagine how her cousin felt. While the pair was charged with keeping the gate safe, it was Anna who held the duty of opening the doorway between realms, and thus sent others away never to return.

"You girls ok out there?" Abbi's mother's voice from inside the house rang out again.

"Yes, momma." It snapped her back to the here and now, and seemed to have done the same for Anna, too. Smiles returned to their faces, questions of the past fled their minds, and they returned to the simple play of children poolside on a nice sunny day.

Boogey Blues

by

Sianyn Leigh

The SUV rumbled along the dirt road, turning onto a narrow driveway marked only by a rough-hewn sign with the name Bartlett painted in bright orange. Jake, slumped forlornly in the backseat, pressed his face against the window and sighed as his family's vacation cabin came into view, hot breath of disappointment fogging the cool glass.

He'd begged his dad to go anywhere else on vacation, even nowhere at all, anyplace but the family cabin. It hadn't done any good.

"Family tradition," he'd insisted.

Well, Jake had learned early in his nine years the *family tradition* seemed to be his cousins making him miserable every time the family gathered together, with the so-called adults blissfully unobservant. He wanted to enjoy his time away from school just once, even if that was only sitting alone in his room watching streaming videos and eating pizza snack rolls. Just one summer to not worry about frogs in his underwear, or worms in his dinner, or shaving cream in his shoes.

Dread balled in the pit of his stomach as the cabin came into view, the extended Bartlett family vehicles filling the driveway. He could see his Aunt Jenny on the porch talking with Uncle David and Papaw Earl. In the yard, his cousins Harvey, Martin, and Mack tumbled over the grass in an imitation of a wrestling match. Jake sank lower into his seat, wishing he could disappear before they saw him.

"Oh, my God, Mom!" His older sister Sadie whined, fingers furiously tapping at the screen of her smartphone. "There's no service out here. How am I supposed to chat with my friends while I'm stuck in the boonies?"

"Try living in analog, Sadie," Mom quipped back, looking over her shoulder briefly to smirk at her frustrated teenager.

Sadie growled in irritation and stared out the window in a pout. From her carseat between her older siblings, four-year-old Hazel strained against her restraints.

"Can I get up yet? My butt hurts."

"Almost" Dad promised, pulling in behind Uncle David's extra-wide, extra-long, extended cab pickup truck. "Ok, we're here!"

No sooner had the words left his mouth than Sadie was out the car, pulling her backpack from behind her seat and tromping away. Hazel wiggled out of her seat straps and slid out the door, taking off for the porch on short, spindly legs. Jake hesitated, unwilling to face the torment his cousins had surely been planning all year.

"Hazel, don't wander off. Sadie, come help unload," Mom shouted, opening the rear hatch of the SUV.

"Can't," Sadie called back. "I'm going to hang with Myra. In *analog*."

Jake watched as his sister trotted over to the picnic table where their older cousins, Myra and Leila, sat. From several feet away, Harvey—a full 5'6 and 160 pounds at fourteen—tackled Mack, who'd just turned seven. He pinned the smaller boy to the ground and twisted his leg up in a hold Jake had seen pro-wrestlers do. Mack screamed and wiggled, unable to pull himself out from under the much larger boy's weight, and begged for mercy. On the porch, Aunt Jenny and Uncle David didn't so much as glance up from their admiration of Hazel's newest invented dance moves.

"Come on, Jake," Mom said, pulling a couple of overnight bags from the back of the SUV and passing them to Dad. "Go play with your cousins. You haven't seen them since Christmas."

Jake sighed and slowly got out of the car. It wouldn't help to argue now. His parents always brushed aside his concerns, told him he was being too sensitive. Socializing is good for you, they'd say. He'd much rather socialize with kids who didn't try to drown him in the toilet bowl. At least they'd only be staying four days this year. Dad had to get back to the office for some big project and couldn't take a whole week off like usual.

"I can help you and dad get the stuff inside," he offered, hoping to delay the inevitable as long as possible.

"That's ok, honey, you go on and play."

He shuffled towards the grappling boys like his feet were made of lead. Martin noticed his approach first, alerting the other two so that by the time Jake came within reach, all three of them had flanked him like wolves after a wounded deer.

"Hey, it's Baby Jakey! You look even smaller than last year," Harvey snickered, eliciting a guffaw from Martin.

"Yeah, did you get smaller?" Martin's toadying to Harvey reminded Jake of a sniveling henchman to a comic book villain. But what he lacked in creativity he had more than once proved he made up for in brute force.

"I'm still growing," Jake mumbled, struggling to keep his face neutral. He didn't dare match insult to insult. He'd learned long ago that any attempt to snap back never went well for him.

"Still growing," Harvey repeated, chuckling again. "Hey, you know, I joined the wrestling team this year and I need to practice my moves. Martin here is too big to do any of the good moves and Mack is too little. Mom would kill me if he got hurt. But, uh, you're about the right size. What do ya say, Jakey? Let me practice my suplex?"

Jake didn't know what a suplex was, but he'd seen Mack begging for mercy not five minutes ago and he had no desire to trade places.

"Yay!" Mack cheered, grinning like a conniving gremlin. "Smash him! Like in a cage match!"

Harvey took a step forward and Jake deftly stepped to the side, fully alert. "I don't think we should practice right now. It's probably not safe on the ground. I mean, they use big mats in real matches, right?"

"It's not a real match," Harvey argued. "It's just practice."

"Just practice," Martin parroted.

"Don't be scared," Harvey continued, taking another step towards him.

Martin squawked and flapped his arms like a chicken, taking a few steps to Jake's right to block any attempt to escape in that direction. Jake glanced towards the porch and the safety of the adults, hoping at least one of them would notice the impending tragedy. No one looked over. Sadie likewise was engrossed in whatever Myra and Leila were talking about, and she never really took his side in anything anyway. He was on his own. There was only one option left.

Without trying to reason with Harvey any further, Jake spun on his heel and ran. Past the line of cars, past the side of the cabin, and straight into the woods behind the property. The sound of the trio thundering after him lent a burst of speed to his legs. He turned off the walking trail and into the brush, jumping over tree debris and tangles of weeds.

"Jakey, get back here. You're not supposed to leave the trail," Harvey yelled after him.

Getting in trouble for leaving the path was a far preferable fate than becoming Harvey's practice dummy. Jake pushed on, ducking under low branches, sneakers slipping on the loamy mounds that rose up between bushes and vines. Harvey called again, followed by Martin's tinny voice and Mack's plaintive pleas for them to wait for him, but Jake didn't slow his pace.

Eventually, his legs ran out of steam and Jake slid into the gap between a large bush and a gnarled, thick tree. Panting, moisture from the ground seeping through the knees of his jeans, Jake listened, waiting for Harvey and Martin to come trundling into view. But the woods were silent, and Jake noticed for the first time just how dim the light had become. The sun barely reached through the thick foliage overhead, and the shadows were so deep he couldn't always tell what was tree and what was shadow.

That was when he heard it: a sniffling, moaning, mournful sound. It wasn't a sound one of his cousins would ever make. A chill ran down his spine, and he peered out from his hiding spot in search of the source. He'd been so concerned with outrunning his cousins, he'd never thought someone else could be in the woods, too.

The sound was coming from the deep shadows in a cluster of bushes across from him. Slowly, Jake crawled out of his hiding spot and crept slowly towards the bushes. There, just visible in the dim light that barely reached through the brambles, sat a figure no bigger than Jake himself, hunched over with arms wrapped tightly around knobby knees and rocking ever so slightly.

"Hello? Are you okay?" Jake asked, pushing his way through the tangled mass. *His family must be at one of the other cabins and he got lost*, Jake thought as he shifted his legs under him to sit next to the crying figure. "Do you know how to get back home?"

The figure turned towards him. Jake's eyes had adjusted to the low light finally, and he noticed from this much closer vantage point it wasn't another kid at all. In fact, Jake didn't know what it was.

The figure was small and thin, but completely covered in hair, with long thin fingers that ended in sharp points and small, horn-like nubs protruding from the top of its head. The face was not clearly defined in the dimness, but Jake could tell it had unusually large eyes and a wide mouth.

He knew he should be afraid, that he should run back to the family cabin as quick as possible, but he just couldn't muster up any fear. It was just too, well, *sad*.

"Hi, I'm Jake. What's your name?"

The creature slowly unfurled its hunched body and rotated just enough to look at him. Staring at him with impossibly large eyes that shined ever so lightly in the shadows like a cat's eyes, it sniffled back a sob.

"Ah-ah-Auggie," it forced out between hiccups.

"Well, Auggie, why are you crying?"

The creature stared at him silently for several heartbeats before taking a deep breath to say, "My brothers threw me out and won't let me come home until I can be a real Boogeyman."

Jake's eyebrows rose. "Boogeyman?"

"Uh-huh." The creature nodded his head. His voice, though obviously light and high like a child's, was rough and gravelly. "They're all big, scary boogeymen, but I'm still too little. I can't frighten anything, and my teeth are too small to bite with, and my horns are just little nubs, and I'll never be a real Boogey!"

Auggie devolved into sobs once more, tears flowing freely down his hairy cheeks. Jake reached out and patted Auggie's shoulder comfortingly, the wiry fur much like a dog he once had. Thanks to his cousins, Jake knew exactly how Auggie felt.

"That's so unfair. You can't control being small! And I'm sure there's tons of other things you can do. Like, I bet you're smarter than they are, right?"

The tears had subsided some with Jake's support, and Auggie nodded his head.

"Yeah, I'm way smarter," he said around a few lingering sniffles. "And I can hide better."

"See? They're just big dummies," Jake assured him. "I have to deal with big dummies, too. But we won't be small forever," Jake continued. "One day, I'm going to be as tall as my dad, and I bet you'll get bigger, too. You just gotta out-think the bullies until then."

"If you say so," Auggie replied, glancing down at his feet. "It feels like it's taking forever."

Growing up did take forever. Jake couldn't wait until he was as old as Harvey. He bet his cousin wouldn't be able to suplex him then.

The sound of his name echoed through the trees and Jake recognized his dad's voice calling him home. He realized the sun had dropped well below the treeline and dinner was waiting.

Scrambling out of the bush, Jake turned one last time to Auggie. "I have to go, but it was nice meeting you. Don't ever let your brothers see you cry. It just makes them hit you harder."

Auggie nodded sagely and gave a little nod. With an encouraging smile, Jake turned and sprinted back towards the trail and his waiting father.

Like every summer, Jake had to share a room with his cousins. And like every summer, they pulled some cheap prank while he was brushing his teeth in the bathroom. When Jake returned ready for bed, it was to find giant mounds of shaving cream filling both his shoes. Neither Harvey nor Martin had anything clever to say, either, just peals of laughter at Jake's frustration, Mack cackling along for solidarity.

An hour later, all three of them were snoring and Jake was still dabbing wet foam from inside his shoe. The shaving cream didn't hurt anything; his shoes weren't ruined.

But they would take forever to dry on their own, and Jake hated having moist feet.

He was fantasizing about all the ways he could exact revenge if he was bigger and stronger. If he could give as good as he got (*tap*), they'd think twice before pulling another prank on him (*tap*). But those days were forever away (*tap*) and he had several days to go before he was safely back in his own bedroom (*tap*).

The soft, rhythmic tapping wriggled through Jake's subconscious, pulling his attention to the window. The only light this far away from civilization came from the half-moon high in the sky, faintly illuminating the limbs of the tree that grew on that side of the house. Thin branches scraped up and down the window, making a soft tap with every pass. Just above those branches, emitting their own soft, silver glow, were two smaller moons. They blinked.

Jake jumped with a sharp gasp, nearly hurling a shoe at the window reflexively. Then he noticed the hair, the nubby horns, the odd outline that framed the features. It was Auggie tapping at the window with his thin, pointy (claws?) fingers.

With a quick glance to ensure his cousins hadn't been disturbed by his noise, Jake crept over to the window and slowly lifted up the sash.

"Auggie, what are you doing here? It's the middle of the night," Jake hissed, risking another peek over his shoulder. All three of his cousins didn't so much as twitch, still snoring softly.

"You were so nice to Auggie, I thought we could be friends," the strange-looking creature said, but with a lilt that turned it into a question on the last word.

Jake hesitated just a moment, a brief image of what Harvey would do to Auggie if he ever saw him flashing through his mind. Despite being a kid Boogeyman, Auggie had been better to Jake than his cousins ever had. He liked the idea of having a friend so far from home. And besides, even Harvey would think twice before trying to bully something that looked as monstrous as Auggie, wouldn't he?

He stepped back from the window and Auggie slid under the sash, the sharp tips of his fingers and toes clicking ever so slightly as he moved. The Boogeyman wasn't wearing any clothes except a scrap of something that looked like a pair of shorts. The rest of his body was completely covered in fine brown fur, all but his face, which looked like what Jake imagined a Bigfoot would look like if they were real. Of course, until today he didn't think Boogeymen were real, either.

"Were your brothers mean to you when you got home?" Jake asked as Auggie perched on the edge of the bed like a vulture on a rock.

The creature's pointed toenails dug into the blanket and his knees were pushed into his chest, arms dangling to either side. It seemed an impossible posture to maintain balance, yet Auggie didn't so much as sway, the mattress barely dipping under his weight.

The thin, hairy shoulders rose and dipped in a slow shrug. "Only as always," he replied in his harsh whisper.

Jake scoffed. "Same as always? Sounds about right." He lifted his soggy shoe for Auggie to see, then jerked his head to the side to indicate his cousins. "They're at their pranks again, as always. Must have used a whole can of shaving cream, there was so much of it! If I did that, Dad would've tanned my hide, but no one ever says anything to them."

Auggie glanced at the sleeping boys. "They are not punished for their misdeeds?"

Jake snorted again. "Never. *They're just playing*. Or, *boys will be boys*. Or worse, when Dad tells me I just need to toughen up. I wish I could get them back just once."

Auggie cocked his head to the side. "But then, wouldn't that make you bad?"

"Maybe." Jake shrugged. "But, what they do is far worse, so me doing it just once should be allowed. It should be fair."

"Fair?" Auggie repeated slowly. Taking a deep breath, he continued, "In the Boogeyland, there isn't any fair. You do bad, then you are bad. Messy, disobedient, troublemaking, staying up too late. Things moms and dads tell you not to do. But if you are good, the Boogeyman doesn't get you."

Jake's brows furrowed. "But, sometimes good people do something bad, even by accident. They forget to clean, or don't know the rules. What if someone is mostly good, but does a little bad?"

Auggie thought for a moment, odd-looking face turning up to the ceiling. His head snapped back down and he declared, "Then, they only get a little bite."

"Bite?" Jake repeated, eyes wide. "You bite people? Like, for real?"

The creature shrugged. "My brothers do all the time. I can't, yet - Auggie teeth are still growing. See?"

Auggie leaned forward, lips pulled back to expose two rows of tiny but needle-sharp teeth. They reminded Jake of cat teeth, which sparked a thought in his mind.

"Hey, Harvey's really bad, and Boogeymen bite when people are bad, right?" Auggie looked dubious, but nodded. "Then, you can get revenge for me. He messed with my shoes, so we can mess with his!"

Jake slid off the bed and shuffled over to the closet all three boys shared. He came back a moment later with one of Harvey's sneakers and thrust it under Auggie's nose. Auggie rocked dangerously back on his heels, teetering on the barest edge of the mattress, and took the offered shoe.

"You want Auggie to *bite* his shoe?"

Jake looked over his shoulder, assuring himself his cousins were still asleep. The steady, snoring rhythm continued without so much as a hitch.

"Yeah, I mean, you can't bite *Harvey*. You could just chew it a little, just enough to be annoying. You know," Jake shrugged, "like what he did to me."

Auggie looked down at the shoe, hesitating. "That doesn't seem good to Auggie. It seems like bad for bad."

"No," Jake shook his head. "It's not. It's punishment for his misdeeds. None of the adults ever do anything, so it's left to us. We have to teach him a lesson." Auggie seemed unconvinced, his face twisted up in thought. Jake scrambled for an excuse the creature could believe. "It's practice for being a real Boogeyman, for when you're all grown up."

That was exactly the push Auggie needed. He smiled and nodded. "Yes, Jake is helping Auggie become a real

Boogeyman, so I will help Jake get back at the bad cousins."

The elation filled Jake as he watched Auggie sink his sharp little teeth into the tongue of the sneaker and begin to gnaw. He could practically levitate for joy. Finally, Harvey was going to get some of his own medicine.

"Mom! Something ate my shoes!"

Jake could barely contain a gleeful chuckle when Harvey woke up to find the tongues on both his shows nothing but shreds. Auggie had nibbled at Martin's shoes, too, leaving both boys with mangled footwear. Mack hadn't been spared either, though by the time Auggie got to the littlest pair, his jaw was sore from all the gnawing. He'd only managed to rip the laces a little, which Jake felt was enough since Mack was only a little annoying.

Aunt Jenny appeared to examine the shoes, then called for Uncle David. After both adults had rummaged around in the closet for a bit, finding nothing but bits of shoe, Uncle David declared a possum or raccoon must have gotten into the house. Harvey begged Uncle David to take him somewhere for a new pair of shoes, but it was two hours to the nearest town. Uncle David didn't want to take a whole day out of his vacation just so Harvey could run around in the mud in new shoes. Instead, he found a roll of duct tape in the kitchen and taped the top of the shoes to Harvey's and Martin's ankles.

Jake didn't feel the least bit guilty laughing as they tromped around in half-taped sneakers, the loose fit causing Martin to trip and land face first in the dirt more than once. In fact, Jake rather enjoyed being able to run faster than his cousins for once.

His small act of revenge filled Jake with a new confidence he'd never felt before. He wanted to try again, just to hold on to that feeling a little longer.

The perfect opportunity presented itself that afternoon. He had gone into the kitchen to get a drink. Aunt Jenny was making cupcakes in preparation for Papaw Earl's birthday tomorrow. Mack came in a moment later and stuck his finger directly into the batter bowl while Aunt Jenny's back was turned. Jake would never have dared such a thing on Aunt Jenny's watch. She could be fearsome when angry. So he watched, pouring his lemonade comically slowly into a short glass so he could see if Mack got away with stealing a nibble.

"Mack!" Aunt Jenny chastised when she caught sight of him. "Keep your hands out of that. Those are for tomorrow."

Mack didn't show the least bit of fear at his mother's scolding. "But, I'm so hungry," he whined, face scrunched up like he was about to cry. "Dinner is too far away!"

"Have some chips."

Aunt Jenny disappeared into the small pantry on the other side of the room. Mack sighed heavily, rolling his eyes, then noticed Jake watching him.

"What are you staring at, freak? Go creep somewhere else before I make Harvey punch you."

"I'm leaving, okay?" Jake promised, walking around the kitchen island to put the lemonade back in the fridge.

Mack turned his back on Jake, lifting his knees onto the counter to reach the bag of chips in the high cabinet, the fabric of his shorts just brushing the bowl of cupcake batter. Keeping his eye on Mack so as not to get caught, Jake surreptitiously snaked an arm over the open fridge door and pressed a fingertip to the edge of the mixing bowl until it slipped from the counter. He closed the door and spun away quickly as the bowl bounced on the floor, splattering batter over the tiles, the cabinets, the island, and even a bit on his shoes. Mack slipped down from the counter at the sound, mouth gaped in horror as Aunt Jenny came running back from the pantry.

"Mackintosh Alexander Wilson! What did I just say about leaving that batter alone. Now look what you've done!"

Her face was a mask of motherly rage. She grabbed the bag of chips from Mack's hand and pulled him by the arm to the sink as he protested, "It was an accident!"

Jake snickered, drawing Mack's eye. "Ask Jake what happened. He was right next to me, I bet he did it!"

Jake forced his eyelids as wide open as they would go, letting his eyes water at the strain, and adopted a wounded look. "I was just putting the juice away, Aunt Jenny. I don't know what Mack was doing with the bowl."

If possible, Mack looked even more shocked at Jake's refusal to back him up. He tried to protest, but Aunt Jenny knew what a troublemaker she had on her hands and wasn't having any of it.

"Listen here, Mister, you're damn lucky I bought extra boxes or you'd be explaining to Papaw why he's not getting a birthday celebration tomorrow. Now, you're going to clean this mess up and I better not hear a peep out of you."

Jake let a smile spread, watching as Mack was condemned to clean the entire kitchen of every last smear of batter and banned from his electronics for the rest of the night. Things were finally looking up for him. He couldn't wait to tell Auggie, and plan their next revenge prank.

That night, Jake stayed up waiting for the sharp tap-tap of Auggie's arrival. He pulled open the sash almost immediately, startling Auggie with his immediate response. The boogeyman leaned against the window frame, greeting Jake with a toothy smile.

"Is nice to see Jake again," Auggie said, his voice deeper than Jake remembered, but just as gravelly. The creature's arms were longer than he remembered, too, the shoulders almost broader than the windowpane and eyes as big as saucers.

"Hey, Auggie, glad you came over. I've got a great idea for tonight," Jake whispered in a rush, ignoring the jolt of unease his friend's changed appearance gave him. "Meet me downstairs."

He shut the window before Auggie had a chance to reply, tiptoeing out of the room and sneaking down the creaky stairs with a shirt clutched in his hand. He opened the back kitchen door and beckoned for Auggie to come inside. The young boogeyman hesitated a moment, then slowly stepped first one furry, clawed foot into the kitchen, and then the other. He straightened as Jake closed the door behind him, several inches taller than he had been only yesterday.

"Oh, wow, you're growing fast," Jake said. "Is that a Boogey thing?"

Auggie looked his friend up and down and gestured at the ill-fitting pajama top he was wearing, the fabric straining at the shoulders. "Jake grow fast, too."

"What? Oh, no. This is Martin's. Here, I brought you one of Harvey's to wear." He handed the shirt in his hand to Auggie. The creature took it, holding it gently between his claws like he was afraid he'd break it. Jake gestured at the shirt. "Put it on. It's part of tonight's plan."

The boogeyman did as he was told. "Plan? Jake not just talk with Auggie?" he asked, voice muffled as he struggled to pull his head through the top. "Auggie like talking."

"We're gonna do something much better than talking." Jake guided Auggie over to the counter, where thirty-six cupcakes with little Happy Birthday flags sat in perfect rows in a covered tray. "We're going to eat all these cupcakes, as messy as we can."

Auggie rolled his big eyes from Jake to the cupcakes, and back again. "Why?"

Jake huffed in frustration. "Because it will get Harvey and Martin in trouble. That's why we're wearing their shirts. We're going to get frosting and crumbs all over them, then I put them back in the laundry pile and when Aunt Jenny finds them tomorrow AND all the cupcakes gone, my cousins are gonna get it for sure."

Auggie didn't seem to share Jake's glee at the plan, looking at him in a mix of disappointment and doubt. At least, that's how Jake interpreted the expression that contorted the oddly-shaped face.

"Were not the shoes enough? Auggie not like getting others in trouble."

"But they're mean to me all the time," Jake whined. "They deserve this. And you said real Boogeymen get revenge on bad kids. You want to be a real Boogeyman, don't you?"

"Auggie does." He sighed, hairy shoulders slumping. "Auggie help."

"Good. You get that half, and I'll take this half."

Twenty-three cupcakes later, neither Jake nor Auggie could eat another bite. Brightly colored frosting stained their shirts and crumbs littered the floor. Auggie gave the borrowed shirt back to Jake and slipped away into the night while Jake tiptoed back upstairs and planted the evidence on top of the laundry basket. He slid into bed grinning ear to ear, dreaming about all the wonderful ways Aunt Jenny and Uncle David were going to punish his cousins when they woke up in the morning.

It was glorious. Phones were confiscated. Wi-Fi privileges were removed. Groundings for literal weeks were declared. Enough chores to qualify as child labor were assigned. Any attempt to protest their punishment only resulted in harsher sentences for obvious lying. Even little Mack wasn't spared by virtue of association, though Uncle David only made him put the dishes away after lunch. Even Papaw gave a long, anger-infused lecture on how disappointed he was in the boys for ruining his 75th birthday.

Jake had never felt so vindicated in his life. After all the summers and family holidays being at their mercy, his cousins were finally getting a taste of their own medicine. Why hadn't he thought to do this earlier? Auggie, of course. Jake would never have the courage to set Harvey and Martin up if he didn't have a real life monster as his friend to back him up. He couldn't wait to tell his friend his mission of revenge was finally done and they could just talk now, just like Auggie wanted.

Hoping to find him near the bush they first met, Jake headed for the woods after Papaw's BBQ buffet had been cleaned away and the adults had wandered back inside to relax in the air conditioning. Dad always took an afternoon nap after a big meal, so he knew he had a couple hours before anyone missed him.

He was surprised to find Harvey and Martin at the rear of the cabin, poking a stick at what Jake assumed was a snake or a frog, or some other hapless creature.

"Hey, Jakey," Harvey said when he noticed him. "You out here all alone?"

Jake stopped, reluctant to let them see which way he was going so he couldn't be followed, knowing Auggie didn't want to be seen by anyone else.

"What are you guys doing here? Didn't You get grounded?"

"Dad said he didn't want us underfoot while the adults are talking," Martin complained, tossing his stick aside with a huff. "No phones, no games. Can't even sit inside where it's cooler. This sucks."

Jake shrugged. "Well, guess you shouldn't have been bad."

Harvey narrowed his eyes. "What about you, Jakey? Have you been bad? Cuz I didn't eat those cupcakes, and I know Martin didn't. Only person left is you."

"Me?" Jake choked, taking a step to the side. "How could I have done it? I couldn't eat that much by myself. And besides, it was your clothes that had frosting all over them."

"You coulda grabbed them, I don't know," Harvey snapped. "You're always sneaking around, trying to look innocent, but I know you've been up to something. Stuff like this never happens when you're not around."

Jake scoffed, trying to look offended. "That sounds silly. You can't prove I did anything."

"No, but I can make you confess," Harvey retorted darkly. "I'll make you regret you were ever born unless you go tell Mom right now Martin and I didn't do it."

"I can't. She wouldn't believe me anyway," Jake argued, stalling for time as he took another step to the side. This encounter could have only one outcome. His only hope was finding Auggie in the woods before Harvey could catch him and make good on his threat.

"Get him!" Harvey shouted, leaping forward and making a grab for Jake's shirt.

Twirling out of reach, Jake dropped into a run, darting into the trees with Harvey and Martin close behind. He followed the same trail he'd gone down a couple days ago, jumping off the path when he recognized a familiar tree. Harvey shouted for Jake to stop or else, galvanizing Jake to run even faster, shouting for Auggie to help him as he jumped over logs and crashed through underbrush.

A dark shape suddenly loomed before him, too close to avoid, and Jake slammed into a solid, fur-covered mass. He heard Harvey and Martin stumble to a stop as he fell to the ground, elbow landing hard in a patch of exposed dirt.

"What is that?" Harvey cried. Jake could hear Martin's high-pitched screech as he looked up at the dark shape and realized with a shock he was staring at Auggie. Taller, broader, with sharper teeth and longer claws, but unmistakably Auggie.

"Jake call for Auggie?" he asked in a voice like metal over concrete. Horns, real horns and not just tiny nubs, protruded from the wayward shanks of hair on his head, and his front teeth had grown into prominent fangs.

"How does that thing know your name?" Harvey asked, voice trembling noticeably, Martin clutching at the bigger boy's arm and ducking behind him.

Jake sighed in relief. He might have gotten even bigger, but he was still Auggie, still his friend. Harvey would have to leave him alone now.

"Auggie, they're trying to hurt me. Do some Boogeyman stuff and make them stop."

The giant moon eyes looked even sadder than they had the night before as they slid over to glare at the two cowering boys. Auggie didn't move, but that look alone was enough to send Harvey and Martin scrambling back. They turned and ran back for the cabin, calling for Aunt Jenny and Uncle David to save them.

With a growl of frustration, Jake spun on Auggie. "Why didn't you scare them? Isn't that what Boogeymen do?"

"They were scared," Auggie replied, blinking down at Jake. "Isn't Jake scared?"

"What? No! They were going to hurt me and you didn't do anything," Jake continued angrily. "I thought you were my friend!"

"Auggie is friend. Boys did not hurt Jake."

"But they were going to!"

"Jake is friend, but does not understand the Boogeyman way," Auggie replied slowly. "Boogeyman does not punish what *might* happen, only what has been done. The boys did not hurt Jake, but Jake has hurt Auggie."

"Hurt you?" Jake chortled. "How have I hurt you?"

"Jake make Auggie break shoes. Jake make Auggie eat too much sugar, hurt Auggie belly. Jake not be good friend to Auggie. Jake bad."

The light in the creature's eyes seemed to dim and Jake suddenly realized just how much bigger than him Auggie had become. The Boogeyman took a shuffling step towards him, reaching one hand with its incredibly long, incredibly sharp claws towards him. Jake's blood turned cold as fear gripped him. In that moment, he wasn't sure Auggie was his friend anymore, but he was sure he wanted to be back in the safety of the cabin, surrounded by his parents and his family.

With a sob, Jake stumbled back and turned, running for the path and the security of four walls and his parents' arms.

Despite his pleading to let him stay in their room, Jake's mom and dad insisted he sleep in the room with his cousins. He wasn't afraid of Harvey and Martin—who were still so shaken by their encounter in the woods they hadn't said anything to Jake since he returned—but rather what would happen if Auggie came by the window tonight.

Reluctantly, Jake settled into his small bed, pulling the cover all the way up to his chin and staring at the window, unable to sleep. The sound of his cousins snoring had gone on for what seemed like hours when his worst fear came to be.

With the sliver of moon high in the sky, the faint silhouette of long, thin fingers and the soft scrape of nails on glass sent chills all the way to his toes. He watched, wide-eyed, as the fingers moved slowly down the pane of glass, then slipped under the edge of the windowsill and lifted ever so slowly.

First one arm, then another reached through the opening, followed by a scruffy, horned head and bulky shoulders. In moments, a shadow made of sharp points and long limbs loomed over Jake's bed.

"Au-Auggie? Is that you?" Jake whispered, trembling.

"Hello, Jake."

"Are you still my friend? Cuz I'm still yours. We can just talk if you want." Jake glanced over at the bed across the room, hoping Harvey, or Martin, or even Mack would wake and sound the alarm. He couldn't do it himself. No matter how he tried, he couldn't force his voice above a whisper.

"Auggie will thank Jake for helping him become a real Boogeyman. Jake was nice when other Boogeys wouldn't speak to Auggie. But Auggie and Jake can't be friends anymore. Jake is bad."

"No." Hot tears welled up in his eyes, running in thick drops down his cheeks. "I'm not bad. I just wanted to teach them a lesson."

"Jake disobey parents by going off the path. Jake destroy property, make a mess, lie, stay up late. Jake do all things parents say not to do."

"But, I only did it because they're always so mean to me and I wanted to get them back, just once." Couldn't Auggie see it wasn't his fault? He had to do something, or the bullying would never stop.

"If cousins mean, then Boogeymen would get them. But, Auggie only ever see Jake be mean. Boogeyman cannot punish for what might happen, only what has happened."

"Please, Auggie. I'll never do anything bad ever again. I promise. Don't punish me, please."

The fur-covered face softened and his lips pulled up over his fangs in a smile. "Auggie believe Jake. And very grateful. Now Auggie real Boogeyman. Auggie can finally bite."

The creature's bottom jaw dropped and long fingers wrapped tightly around Jake's arms, the razor-sharp nails cutting into his flesh. Jake opened his mouth to scream, but still it only came out as a whisper.

About the Authors

DANA LOCKHART

Dana Lockhart grew up on the outskirts of a town of 199 people, but the small-town life couldn't contain her spirit. She yearned for something more adventurous and worthwhile, and, more than anything, for her voice to be heard.

After completing her degree, she went out into the world to try and make a name for herself, but she's still trying to find out where she belongs. She has since sought careers in helping others, including in local government, non-profits, and legal services. Her proudest achievement is being elected the first vice president of the Hannibal

Writers Guild in 2018, and later the president in 2019. In addition, she is a public speaker and art hobbyist.

Dana Lockhart primarily writes urban fantasy, ranging from young adult to adult. She's also been known to write a short story or poem now and then. At the time of writing, she has two books published: an urban fantasy novel *The Un-Life of William Moore*, and a poetry collection, *In the Deluge*.

She lives a modest life on the banks of the Mississippi River with her two cats, Nimble and Binx.

Website: www.danalockhart.com

Email: danalockhart411@gmail.com

ASHLEY WONG

Ashley Kay Wong is a best-selling fantasy author. She runs a blog called Clever & WTF with her sister, where they both share their fantasy and speculative fiction stories. When she is not writing, she spends time with her husband and her rescue dog, Bailey. Ashley is a coffee addict with a fondness for cozy games. While she uses her passion for justice as a Victim Advocate, she also enjoys writing daring female characters who fight against injustice in their own world. You can read more of her stories at cleverandwtf.com and connect with her on Facebook at www.facebook.com/ashleykaywong.

KIM ZIERES

Kim is a registered nurse by day and an integral part of Chaos and Ink all the other times. She was first published in the Good Nonsense anthology collection from the Hannibal Writers Guild in August 2024, is the Vice President and assistant editor for the Hannibal Writers Guild, and mom to four mostly-grown children.

Having grown up in the same semi-rural town, Kim has found creative outlets wherever she can, including collaborating on scripting a play, performing stage comedies, and filming a never-to-be-seen music video.

Kim spends her free time penning her next fantastic tale or online gaming.

AMBER LEIGH

Amber has been sharing her writing on Clever & WTF, the website she runs with her sister, since 2019. While she primarily writes fantasy, she occasionally dabbles in other genres and prefers writing darker stories. You can explore more of her writing at cleverandwtf.com. Amber lives in Wisconsin with her partner and their furry companion, Appa the malamute.

Marie C. Erikson

Marie C. Erikson was told by her elementary school teachers that she was "such a good writer!" She forgot about this during high school and didn't remember it again until over a decade later when she was in graduate school for psychology and she noticed her professors were commenting "Well written!" on her research papers. This is when it finally occurred to her to try writing something other than school assignments. In addition to being a poetry and fantasy writer, Marie is sometimes a behavioral health social worker and always a nerd. She lives in Illinois with her children.

SARAH TOLLOK

Sarah Tollok lives in the beautiful Shenandoah Valley of Virginia with her husband and two sons. Her work can be found in anthologies with Improbable Press, Alan Squire Publishing, Clan Destine Press, and Memento Vivere Press. *Bookstories*, the author's love letter to the world of books, was released in 2024 with Balance of Seven Press. You can find out more about her work at SarahTollok.com.

Don't Step in Fairy Rings Bio

JAY LEVY

A devoted writer of genre fiction and role-playing games, Jay spends much of his free time reading stacks of comic books, and taking walks with his lovely shield-maiden wife and dogs.

His other works can be found in *Beneath the Yellow Lights, I Used to be an Animal Lover, Dark Halloween, Scary Snippets: Valentine's Day, Scary Snippets: Halloween, Scary Snippets: Christmas, Scary Snippets: Virtual, Fatal Fairies, A Guide to Useless Sidekicks,* and *Guilty Pleasures and Other Dark Delights.* To contact, please visit: https://jaylevy.substack.com/

SIANYN LEIGH

Fantasy author Sianyn Leigh grew up reading old fairy tales at her grandmother's knee, instilling in her a passion for history, mythology, and the importance of story-telling. Obsessed with the rich pantheons, folklore, and superstitions across the world, she enjoys exploring the "what ifs" of life's many questions and weaving them into fanciful tales.

Infinitely more entertained by a rich fantasy life than reality, Sianyn has embarked upon a journey of sharing her musings with the world in the hopes others may also be entertained. She founded Chaos and Ink Books in early 2024 and hopes to provide tomes upon tomes of entertainment to readers for years to come.

Sianyn interned with a senior editor for two years assisting with clients and copywriting, and completed a writing course from the University of Queensland. She currently squeezes writing time and business operations around her day job in Medical Billing.

When not writing or working, you can find Sianyn binge-watching her favorite TV shows, entertaining two energetic dogs, and sleeping.

ROB GOODALE

Rob E. Goodale has written and edited fiction for small-market and independent publishers since 2015 under several different pen names.

A lifelong learner, his day job as a freelance copywriter and content writer lets him revel in the written word while helping businesses engage their audiences.

When not working or writing, he's pursuing a Bachelor of the Arts in Philosophy, and you may trip across him in either Azeroth or Eorzea.

www.ingramcontent.com/pod-product-compliance
Lightning Source LLC
Chambersburg PA
CBHW031051310726
48969CB00007B/2221